RYDER O'NEAL—PAX

1. Call Moscow
2. Fax White House
3. Meeting at the U.N.
4. Save the world
5. Fall in love

Just another day at the office...

MEN at WORK

✈—MILLIONAIRE'S CLUB   🍎—BOARDROOM BOYS   🔆—MAGNIFICENT MEN

🔧—TALL, DARK & SMART   🛡—DOCTOR, DOCTOR   🥾—MEN OF THE WEST

🕴🏼—MEN OF STEEL   🛡—MEN IN UNIFORM

MEN at WORK

BARBARA BRETTON

PLAYING FOR TIME

MEN
IN
UNIFORM

Harlequin Books

TORONTO • NEW YORK • LONDON
AMSTERDAM • PARIS • SYDNEY • HAMBURG
STOCKHOLM • ATHENS • TOKYO • MILAN
MADRID • WARSAW • BUDAPEST • AUCKLAND

HARLEQUIN BOOKS
225 Duncan Mill Road, Don Mills,
Ontario, Canada M3B 3K9

ISBN 0-373-81058-X

PLAYING FOR TIME

Copyright © 1987 by Barbara Bretton

This edition published by arrangement with Harlequin Books S.A.

® and TM are trademarks of the publisher. Trademarks indicated with
® are registered in the United States Patent and Trademark Office, the
Canadian Trade Marks Office and in other countries.

Printed in U.S.A.

Dear Reader,

It's June 1986 and our Long Island house is up for sale. The first floor is swarming with Realtors. I'm upstairs in my office, working on this book, engrossed in the adventures of Ryder and Joanna and PAX, when I hear voices.

"What do you think she's doing?" Realtor #1 whispers.

"I don't know," says Realtor #2. "Typing, I think."

"Look at those pictures on the wall," says #1. "Are they book covers?"

"Maybe she types manuscripts," says #2. "She's fast enough."

I can't help but turn around and smile at them. "I'm a writer," I say proudly. "Those are my book covers on the wall."

"Get out of here," says Realtor #1. "You are not!"

"Yes, I am," I say. "See—that's my name on the covers."

Every now and again the sun shines down on you, and this was my day. The house didn't sell any faster, but I was definitely a VIP that day. Twenty-two Realtors watched me write a few paragraphs—none of which made it into the book.

So far, I've written seven books about my band of merry PAX spies: *Playing for Time*, *Honeymoon Hotel*, *A Fine Madness*, *All We Know of Heaven*, *The Bride Came C.O.D.*, *Operation: Husband* and the upcoming *Operation: Family*. I have a special place in my heart for this one that started it all.

Barbara Delton

Age is like love, it cannot be hid.
—Thomas Dekker: *Old Fortunatus* II.i

With Love:
To Doctor T and Minnehaha,
who are still waiting for
Concierge Ken to call back
and
To Mona and the girls,
aka The Terrors of Pompano Beach

Chapter One

Ryder O'Neal swore as he rearranged his right leg on top of the mahogany table in front of the couch. The cast was heavy and hot and it itched like hell, and after six weeks of imprisonment Ryder was at the end of his rope.

Alistair Chambers's urbane laughter was just about enough to send him over the edge.

"Better watch it, Chambers," Ryder said, waving his crutch aloft. "This can be a dangerous weapon."

The older man folded his slim, impeccably tailored frame into a chair close to the couch.

"Courting danger is my forte," he said, his voice revealing his British origin. "I am ever fearless." He handed Ryder a glass of Scotch.

The drink warmed its way down Ryder's throat and mellowed his mood despite himself. "What you are," he said, "is a royal pain in the—"

"Save your American vulgarisms for someone else," Alistair broke in. "I am impervious to such blatant ploys for sympathy."

"I don't want sympathy. I want my freedom."

Alistair made a show of looking around the elegantly appointed apartment. Except for the stacks of notes on the desk and the mass of electronic equipment locked away in the two spare bedrooms, the place was straight out of *Architectural*

Digest. "I see no bars at the windows, my boy, and no shackles upon your wrists."

Ryder pointed toward the heavy cast on his right leg. "Who needs shackles when the prisoner has a fractured femur?"

"Six weeks ago you didn't know what a femur was."

"Six weeks ago I didn't need to know what a femur was."

"This is right and just punishment for carousing on that godforsaken mountain in Vermont. A more sensible man would have amused himself with diversions of a different nature."

Ryder drained his drink and put the glass down on the windowsill behind him. "Like that blonde I saw you with after the summit meeting?" The state of Vermont had recently played host to a U.S.-U.S.S.R. summit meeting on combating global terrorism, a topic with which both men were well versed.

Alistair arched one supremely elegant brow. "Dare I mention the brunette who signed your cast with a rather interesting, if physiologically unlikely, proposition?"

"That proposition was in Hebrew," Ryder said. "Isn't there one damned language you can't read?"

"I can decipher double entendres in eighteen modern languages plus Latin and Greek. One never knows when such knowledge will prove useful."

Ryder stretched and yawned theatrically. "Isn't it time you went back to the hotel?"

Alistair crossed his left leg over his right and settled back in his chair. "Would you be trying to rid yourself of my company, my boy? And here I was about to ask you to have dinner with me at O'Shaughnessy's."

O'Shaughnessy's, in Boston, was one of the more popular watering holes of the cloak-and-dagger set and an easy hop in the organization's private jet.

Heavy-duty bribery was hard for Ryder to ignore when he'd been staring at the same four walls all day, but he'd make a valiant attempt. He turned on the television with the remote control device. The theme music from *General Hospital* filled the room. If that didn't drive Alistair—good-natured snob that he was—out of the apartment, nothing would.

To Ryder's dismay, Alistair seemed oblivious to the barrage of diaper and soap powder commercials that followed the opening credits. The older man took a long sip of his own drink then fixed Ryder with one of his patented upper-crust looks.

"Your plebeian pursuits won't drive me out, Ryder, try as you might. I enjoy *General Hospital*."

Ryder zapped through the stations until he reached MTV. He grinned as Alistair winced at the onslaught of heavy-metal music. "Do I see you heading for the door, Chambers?"

Alistair rose from his chair and turned off the TV. He then grabbed the remote control device from Ryder and stashed it in the pocket of his Harris tweed blazer.

"Rudeness in one as brilliant as you can be overlooked occasionally," Alistair said. "But I wouldn't push the boundaries of my largesse."

Ryder sighed and leaned his head against the back of the couch. "Leave me alone, Alistair," he said finally. "I just want out."

The older man walked over to the bar. "And that, dear boy, is the rub." Ryder watched as he poured two more jiggers of Scotch into heavy Baccarat tumblers. "We simply cannot afford to let you go."

"No one is irreplaceable. You can do better."

"Would that we could," Alistair said, handing him a glass. "God knows my life would be simpler with a less demanding resident genius. The fact remains, however, that you are still the best there is."

"I'm burned out."

"Hence this wonderful apartment I've presented you with." Alistair spread his arms wide. "Your personal refuge while you recover your enthusiasm."

Ryder wasn't certain his enthusiasm was recoverable.

The prestigious old Carillon Arms with its vaulted ceilings and marble floors was a Manhattan status symbol. The building was going co-op, and apartments were at a premium since few vacancies existed. Many of the tenants had been there forty or fifty years and, thanks to New York City laws, were protected from eviction but not, unfortunately, from harassment by landlords eager to turn a whopping profit. Some of the stories of harassment Rosie Callahan, a longtime resident, had told Ryder belied the tasteful Carillon exterior.

But then Ryder knew all about false exteriors. You couldn't be in his line of work and not know that things were rarely as they seemed.

Alistair, and the organization, had been exceedingly generous in acquiring one of the pricey apartments for Ryder as a get-well present—a get-well present that came with more than a few strings attached.

"You don't play fair, Chambers." He glared over at his friend and mentor.

"I know. That's the simple beauty of my strategy."

"If I didn't have this damned cast on my leg you'd be in big trouble."

Alistair straightened the left cuff of his Brooks Brothers shirt. "I tremble even as I think of your wrath."

Riders normal good humor was beginning to surface despite himself. "You know what you can do with your British reserve?"

Alistair's blue eyes twinkled. "I already have, my boy. Many times."

Ryder motioned toward the opulent apartment with its cavernous hall and many bedrooms. "You realize even this won't change my mind, don't you? I'm through. Out. Officially retired." Never mind the fact that he'd been spending his idle hours working on a prototype for a device to detect plastic explosives. Chambers didn't need to know everything.

Alistair finished his second Scotch and put the glass down on the highly polished end table. "You're on a leave of absence."

"The hell I am."

"You always say that." Alistair's stiff-upper-lip demeanor

usually amused Ryder. Today it made him crazy. "After each and every job, you say that. I just ignore you."

"You'd better stop ignoring me." Ryder's voice was filled with not-so-righteous anger. "I didn't bargain on a busted leg as part of the deal."

"Oh, come now," Alistair said. "You sound as if you were injured in the line of duty. I have no sympathy for a man who breaks his leg getting off a ski lift."

Ryder chose to ignore the dig.

"You are but thirty-four, Ryder. Certainly you have a few good years left."

Ryder considered the work he'd been doing the past fifteen years. "It's a miracle I made it this far. Why press my luck?"

"Because you'd go slowly mad if you stayed home counting your money." Alistair stood up and walked over to the window overlooking Central Park. "Because it's in your blood just as it's in mine, and you'll never be free of it."

"You always were an optimistic sort." He tried to ignore the uneasy feeling the other man's words brought to life. Memories of the colleagues lost over the years to madmen and geniuses were the most powerful tool in Alistair's arsenal. "I'll check into the Betty Ford Clinic. Maybe they can find a cure."

"There is no cure," Alistair said. "Danger is addictive. Once you get a taste of it, you're hooked."

"I can give it up."

Alistair's expression was a painful mixture of affection and disbelief. "We all want to," he said. "Damned few of us can pull it off."

For the second time in as many days, Ryder thought of Valerie Parker and the life he might have had with her if his ambition hadn't come first, last and always. She was now someone's wife and someone's mother, contentedly hidden away in English suburbia, with Ryder O'Neal just a distant, unhappy memory.

And yet lately Valerie had been popping into his head at odd hours, causing Ryder, never an introspective man, to take

a step backward into his past and face the fact that in this one
thing, he had failed and failed badly.

He carried no torch for her; in fact, he wondered if he'd
ever really loved her at all. Certainly no man who loved could
ever have been so callous, so unfeeling as he had been years
ago.

No. Valerie was now a symbol for something that went far
beyond his shortcomings of the heart: she represented the part
of Ryder that had been ignored during his fifteen years of duty
with PAX.

"Does that invitation to O'Shaughnessy's still hold?" he
asked.

"All it takes is one phone call and we're off."

Ryder grabbed for his crutches and pulled himself up from
the couch.

"Then make the call," Ryder said, "and let's get the hell
out of here."

He'd had a glimpse into his future and he didn't like what
he saw. Not one damned bit.

ON THE NINTH FLOOR of the Carillon, it was the present that
was the problem.

"For heaven's sake, Holland, will you put that stuff
down?" Joanna Stratton grabbed the tube of undereye concealer from her best friend and stashed it in the pocket of her
gray trousers. "You've used enough Erace to camouflage the
entire Sixth Fleet."

"The Sixth Fleet, maybe, but not these circles under my
eyes." Holland pulled another tube of cover-up cream out of
Joanna's enormous makeup kit. "I'm bringing in the rein-
forcements."

Joanna watched Holland add a third layer of Alabaster 1A.
"Who's supposed to be the expert around here anyway? I
thought the idea was to look natural." She groaned as Holland
blended the light concealer with the darker foundation. "You
should have told me you were auditioning for the Kabuki theater."

"I'll ignore the insult if you'll tell me how to cover the dark circles so I don't end up looking like a raccoon." Holland pointed toward the life mask Joanna had done of her a few days ago. "Even that thing has circles under the eyes."

Joanna pulled the makeup kit away from Holland. "Sorry, pal. Trade secret."

"Do you accept bribes?"

"Only if they include dinner at Tavern-on-the-Green and my own Porsche."

"Europe must have agreed with you, darling. Gone only three months and you've become positively autocratic."

"And you've become positively neurotic." Joanna moved aside Holland's life mask and one of Rosie Callahan, her next-door neighbor, and perched on the windowsill next to her mother's antique rolltop desk. Cynthia was in Greece getting to know the latest man in her life and Joanna was availing herself of her mother's rare generosity and vacationing at her Manhattan apartment.

"What on earth is the matter with you?" Joanna asked. "You've been acting strange all morning."

"It's pretty obvious, isn't it?" Holland leaned forward to check the faint laugh lines at the corners of her mouth. "I'm forty-two years old and I'm beginning to look it."

Joanna, a professional makeup artist of some renown, understood beauty and its relationship to aging the way few others did. It was her business to understand the subtle pulls and tugs made by gravity and time and how best to hide them.

When she looked at Holland, she saw a beautiful woman who looked exactly what she was: a woman, not a girl.

"What's wrong with being forty-two? Linda Evans and Stefanie Powers don't seem to mind."

"Neither would I if my career were in high gear the way theirs are," Holland said with a quick laugh. "It's a tough world out there, Joanna, and the older you get, the tougher it gets to survive."

"No wonder you've been troweling on the makeup like camouflage paint. You're preparing for war."

"Laugh all you want. Ten years from now you won't think it's so funny." Holland waved a wand of mascara in her direction. "Just don't come crying to me when you find your first laugh line."

Thirty-two-year-old Joanna bent down so the uncompromising morning sun caught her full face. She pointed toward a few fine lines at the outer corners of her blue-green eyes and the faintest of creases on her forehead.

"Battle scars." She watched Holland's face. "I've had them since I was nineteen." They were vivid reminders of exactly what could happen to a woman when she let herself believe in happily-ever-after.

"You're gorgeous," Holland said matter-of-factly. "You can afford to have a wrinkle or two. It's the rest of us mere mortals who have the problem." She smoothed the furrows on her forehead with an index finger. "Don't you have any potions in your bag of tricks that could make me look ten years younger?"

"Actually I'm looking for a way to add wrinkles."

Holland's expression was priceless. "I'm calling Bellevue."

"You surprise me, Holland. I thought you'd call Bloomingdale's for some industrial strength face cream."

"Be serious. Wrinkles are no laughing matter."

"I am serious. Benny Ryan wants me to do some special effects for a commercial he's shooting next week." Although Joanna was technically on a sabbatical, that didn't keep the offers from pouring in. Saying no hadn't been a problem until Benny's call came in the day before. Disguising a young man as his older self was too fascinating a proposal to ignore.

When it came to disguises, Joanna Stratton was in her element. The more successful she became at creating masks for others, the better the mask she created for herself. In fact, some of her best work was seen every day in the smooth and lovely face she presented to the world.

The struggle to piece her life together after the sudden, violent end of her teenage marriage didn't show. The years of study and apprenticeship, the insecurity and loneliness that were her birthright the same as her beauty—none of these were visible. Not even to her closest friend.

The nomadic life of a free-lance theatrical makeup artist— disguises, a specialty—suited Joanna perfectly. By never staying too long in one place she never ran the risk of growing seriously attached to anything or anyone.

And if lately she'd begun to feel the need for something more tugging and pulling at her coat strings—well, she had only to look at her much-married mother to know how slim her own chances really were for the little cottage with the white picket fence.

It made a hell of a lot more sense for a woman to buy her own little cottage than to wait for Prince Charming to come along and make a down payment. These days, Prince Charmings were in short supply.

The mention of a job possibility had caused Holland to sit up straighter. "Anything in it for me?"

Joanna shook off her pensive thoughts. "Only if you want to play a man who ages fifty years waiting in line for a bank teller."

"Forget it."

"Not even for your art?"

"Not even if it comes with a Tony, an Emmy and an Oscar." Holland shuddered. "Why would you want to take on such a depressing job?"

"I think it's intriguing," Joanna countered. "I've spent the past ten years making septuagenarians look like teenyboppers—why not see if it works the other way around?"

"You're perverse."

"Maybe, but think what fun I'll have." Holland reached for the concealer again and Joanna grabbed it from her. "I could show you how you'll look thirty years from now."

"Bite your tongue!"

"Why this sudden panic over a few laugh lines? You weren't like this when I saw you back in October."

"I wasn't forty-two in October."

"I doubt if your social life has suffered because of it."

Holland always had a string of eligible and not-so-eligible men vying for her favors.

"Well, I haven't joined the Sisters of the Celibate Poor, if that's what you mean."

Joanna ignored the jab at her own currently dull social life. "Level with me, Holland."

Holland sighed. "I need more sleep, more makeup, and a hell of a lot more guts to make it against the competition these days, Jo—both on *and* off the stage." She turned slightly and looked out the window. "And it's scaring the hell out of me."

Joanna was quiet.

She'd spent the past few months in Europe doing the makeup for three top American stars who were filming a mini-series in between temper tantrums and anxiety attacks.

America's insane devotion to youth and perfection had turned three supremely gifted adults into neurotics. However, the fear in Holland's eyes was something else again. It wasn't a performer's fear; it was a woman's fear. A fear Joanna had seen in her mother's eyes, a fear that went deeper than the bone.

"When's the audition?"

"Tomorrow morning." Holland turned the magnifying mirror facedown. "Can you perform a miracle?"

"Let me look at you."

Joanna studied Holland's flawless cheekbones, clear green eyes and thick auburn hair. Laugh lines or no laugh lines, Holland was a classically beautiful woman and was destined to remain one well into old age.

But Joanna knew that was the last thing her friend wanted to hear and the last thing she would believe.

"I don't know," Joanna said with a smile. "It'll be a tough job."

"I'm shameless," Holland said. "You make me beautiful and I'll take you to lunch."

"Tavern-on-the-Green?"

Holland winced. "Would you settle for Jake's on the East Side?"

"You're buying?"

"I'm buying. Miracles don't come cheap."

"You're in luck," Joanna said, reaching for the Pure Beige 004. "Miracles just happen to be my specialty."

Now, if she could just manage a few of her own...

Chapter Two

Jake's turned out to be a marvelous art-deco-style restaurant that made Joanna forget all about Tavern-on-the-Green. She and Holland had a great lunch, then the two women said good-bye at the corner of East 41st and Second Avenue and Joanna took a cab back to the Carillon.

On her way to the elevator, Joanna remembered she hadn't checked for mail in two days so she doubled back toward the mail room off the main lobby. Swinging open the door, she bumped smack into Stanley Holt, the superintendent of the Carillon Arms, who was crouched down beneath the long row of shiny brass mailboxes with his tool kit by his side.

"Miss Stratton! 'Scuse me but I didn't hear you come in." He picked up his battered green cloth tool kit. "I'll get out of your way."

What an odd thing to say, Joanna thought. There was nothing even vaguely unusual about either a tenant fetching her mail or a super performing his duties, but then Stanley always managed to hit just the right note of slippery subservience that set Joanna's teeth on edge.

He brushed off his hands on the legs of his khaki-colored coveralls and stood up. His short, powerfully-muscled body seemed more imposing than usual in the confines of the tiny mail room.

Although he treated her with respect, Joanna detected a certain unmistakable flicker of male interest in his dark brown eyes each time he looked at her, and so she always went out of her way to be scrupulously polite and businesslike and not the slightest bit interested.

"Don't leave on my account, Stanley. I just popped in to get the mail." As if there could be another, more pressing reason for showing up in the mail room at one o'clock in the afternoon.

However, Joanna knew that when dealing with Stanley's type of man, even the obvious had to be made more so.

She rummaged in the pocket of her coat for the tiny mailbox key, searching through loose change and crumpled dollar bills. "I really should take a course in organization," she muttered as her fingers finally closed around her key chain. "One day I'll..."

She looked up and her words died off as she saw two men, just past their teenage years, standing by the open door. Neither one looked familiar. One had longish red hair and bright blue eyes, while the other had close-cropped red hair and brown eyes, the same as Stanley. Both of them were watching her with avid interest.

She turned to Stanley.

"Don't worry about those two, Miss Stratton," he said, picking up a tool from the floor and putting it in his tool kit. "They look like trouble, but they're okay."

"Yeah," said the shorter of the two helpers. "We look like trouble but Stanley keeps us in line."

"I wasn't worried," Joanna lied over the accelerated thumping of her heart. "You just surprised me, that's all."

"They're my new assistants," Stanley said, his dark gaze fastened on the two younger men who lounged in the doorway. "We got a lot more work around here since we went co-op and the boss said I could hire on some help."

Joanna unlocked the mailbox and pulled out *Time*, *People*, a fat bill from New York Telephone and a thin airmail letter from one of her friends in Scotland. "Well," she said, acutely aware of the three men surrounding her, "I'll let you get back to your work." She noticed one of Rosie's fliers, advertising a tenants' meeting, on the floor near Stanley's foot and she bent down to retrieve it.

Stanley motioned quickly with his right hand and the two young men parted like the Red Sea and made room for Joanna to pass. She paused just long enough to tack the flier on the bulletin board opposite the mailboxes.

"You have a good day now, Miss Stratton," Stanley called after her. "You have a real good day."

As Joanna turned the corner toward the elevator she heard the rumble of male laughter and it wasn't difficult to imagine the kind of crude sexual innuendo that had precipitated it.

To hell with Stanley and his pals, she thought as she pushed the button for the ninth floor and the elevator doors slid shut. The Carillon and its employees were Cynthia's problem, not hers.

At the moment, Joanna's most pressing problem was figuring out how she would manage the makeup techniques Benny Ryan's job offer required.

Although she fought Holland every step of the way when it came to aging and its inherent problems, much of what her friend had to say about the subject was painfully on target. Joanna had only to look at her own mother to see that.

Cynthia Hayes Stratton Donato VanDyke del Portago prized beauty and youth above all else and, at the moment, she was enjoying both on a small Greek island with a bronzed giant named Stavros, who was young enough to be Joanna's kid brother.

Cynthia had been chasing the fountain of youth for the past thirty years, stubbornly refusing to believe that nothing could stay the hand of time. Her search had led her through multiple marriages and numerous heartbreaks on five continents while Joanna grew up under the watchful eyes of a series of nannies.

Joanna's search had been for something else entirely. Her father was a dim memory; her mother, a shooting star. The love and guidance her starving heart had craved couldn't be found in the paid affections of housekeepers and baby sitters. The pretty child had turned into a beautiful young woman raised to believe her own happiness was dependent upon the protection of a man.

So it was no surprise that Joanna tumbled into love with the first young man who offered her a way out. Her brief marriage had been the one time in her life when she felt totally loved, totally necessary to another person's happiness. That made Eddie's death—and its shocking aftermath—that much harder to bear. But bear it she did, and in so doing she gained an inner strength that no age spot or laugh line could destroy.

Joanna got out at the ninth floor and let herself into her temporary home, closing the series of locks and bolts securely behind her.

Even though Holland's apprehensions were the direct result of a career that placed as high a value on beauty as it did on talent, Joanna hated to see her friend begin the downward spiral that finally destroyed a woman's self-esteem.

Joanna was sick to death of pretending she could make time stand still, of playing tricks with shadow and light to soothe the blistered egos of stars who'd spent too many years in the Hollywood sun. The years of traveling from place to place, always one step ahead of her loneliness, were beginning to pall. Love might not be on her horizon, but professional satisfaction was within her grasp if she was willing to branch away from the familiar and take a few chances.

The more she thought about it, the more Benny Ryan's offer appealed to Joanna's sense of perverse whimsy. The prestige of fighting the tide of youth intrigued her. Maybe her work would never win the Nobel Peace Prize, but the thought that there was an alternative to discovering the perfect eye shadow applicator was incentive enough.

The question was: Could she pull it off?

She sat down at the desk and set the magnifying mirror in position. Grabbing a headband she scraped her shiny black hair off her forehead and studied her face the way an artist studied a fresh canvas. Large, slightly slanted eyes. Thick, well-defined black brows. Narrow nose. High cheekbones, full mouth. Thanks to Cynthia and good genes, it was a face many directors had felt belonged on the other side of the camera. Joanna, however, valued her privacy too much to expose herself to that uncompromising critic. Now the trick was to take that particular combination of features and project them some forty years into the future.

Paler foundation. Heavy face powder and latex spirit gum to give the appearance of heavy lines beneath her eyes. Her fingers traced the hollows beneath her cheekbones. A fleshier face would be easier to work with. She'd have to remember to tell Benny that when it came time to cast the commercial.

Quickly she daubed on some brown and gray shadows to simulate the effects of age on a woman's skin. She would need a trip to Ranaghan's for supplies if she was going to do this up properly, but she had enough materials at hand right now for a start.

Twenty minutes later Joanna looked into the mirror and saw her future self, circa 2025. The sight was enough to extinguish that lustful light in Stanley's eyes permanently.

But she still hadn't faced the acid test—Central Park West in full early March sunshine surrounded by Yuppies and street people and the usual Wednesday phalanx of ladies-who-lunch who moved up the avenue like a flotilla of mink coats with feet.

If no one handed her a pack of Kleenex and a jar of cold cream, she was in business. And, if they did—well, it would make a great dinnertime topic at Rosie's that evening.

Joanna stuffed her hair into a bright red wool cap she'd bought in Switzerland, grabbed her coat and house keys and set out on a fact-finding mission: Whistler's Mother—in sweatpants and Reeboks—conquers the Upper West Side.

Winner take all.

THE LAUNDRY ROOM of the Carillon Arms reminded Ryder of an old *Odd Couple* episode where Felix and Oscar entertained dates to the accompaniment of soapsuds and liquid fabric softener. Despite the champagne and soft music, romance rarely flourished by the light of the Whirlpool.

Of course, romance was not what the Carillon's management had had in mind when they decorated the laundry room, but they certainly had tried very hard to lift it out of the ranks of the utilitarian and into the exalted realm of high-tech trendiness.

However, not even wall-to-wall carpeting, overstuffed chairs and a soda machine that dispensed both Pepsi and Perrier could hide the fact that whenever you put a washer and dryer in the same room, you meant business.

It was certainly a far cry from the ultraexclusive, ultraexpensive O'Shaughnessy's in Boston, where he'd spent most of the afternoon enjoying lobster and shrimp and some of the best gossip that side of the White House. Alistair had gone all out to lure Ryder into reconsidering his threat to retire from PAX.

Little did Alistair know that last month's trip back home to Omaha had done more to lure Ryder than all of the fancy apartments and private jets PAX could provide. He'd gone back for his niece's christening, expecting to be greeted as the conquering hero, his broken leg a testimony to the glamour and danger inherent in his mysterious profession.

His suburban brothers, whose Bible was *Consumer's Digest* and whose creed was the adjustable-rate mortgage, would gnash their teeth in despair and yearn for days gone by. His sisters, mired in motherhood and drowning in domesticity, would sift through their lists of single friends, wondering if any of them would be sophisticated enough for their world-traveling brother.

Ryder's expectations were well defined.

And none of them was met.

OMAHA HAD CHANGED. That was the first thing Ryder noticed as he drove into town. Where once it had ended around the Westroads Shopping Center, now it sprawled outward and beyond, a great, thriving city unlike the sleepy town he remembered from his childhood.

The old landmarks were still there—the signs to Offutt Air

Force Base, Southroads, the kids from the University of Nebraska at Omaha and Creighton dragging up Dodge Street—but somehow none of them seemed to fit any longer. Progress had swept through Omaha, surrounding Addison's Soda Shop and Swatek's Delicatessen, threatening to engulf them in nationwide chain stores that were the death knell of regionality.

He chuckled as the limo driver turned onto L Street, which headed toward his mother's house. Ridiculous, sentimental thoughts. He'd been born with a passport in his hand, as eager to be free of familial restraints as he'd felt his family eager to see him go. His first memories were of his mother weeping in a dark corner of the bedroom while his father got ready for another night with the boys.

He'd hated his father for the demons that finally drove him out of their lives but Ryder had sensed early on that the placid domesticity that his brothers seemed born to had somehow passed him by. The world outside had called to him and he'd answered that call and never looked back until now.

The limo pulled into the rutted driveway in front of the big white frame house with the black shutters that always managed to look just slightly out-of-whack. *This is it,* he thought as he maneuvered himself and his crutches out of the Lincoln. After two days of being treated as the conquering hero, of fielding his brothers' envious questions and the outright hero worship of his nieces and nephews, he'd be reassured that what he had with PAX was exactly what he wanted.

NOTHING HAD WORKED OUT as planned.

His brothers and sisters understood more about life and happiness than Ryder had ever dreamed of. They had woven their lives into the fabric of community and family, fitting their hopes and dreams into the pattern of continuity. No one wondered about his mysterious profession. No one seemed willing to trade K-Mart and Baker's for the south of France.

They were happy with their lives and with themselves. They were curious about his travels but not envious. Where once he'd believed his brothers to be lacking in daring, now his perception of what constituted daring changed.

What, then, took more courage: facing bullets or facing up to the responsibility of family life? Years ago he would have known the answer. He laughed hollowly and, in that laugh, heard the echo of his father.

Hell. Years ago he wouldn't have asked the question. Time, however, didn't stand still—not even for men like Ryder O'Neal.

He wanted everything, Ryder did. He wanted the excitement of PAX, he wanted the danger and the drama and, now in his thirty-fourth year, he wanted the one thing he'd always turned away from: he wanted love.

Normal men didn't know how to disassemble a Kalashnikov rifle or understand how enough FOAM-X to blow up the World Trade Center could be hidden in a can of shaving cream.

"You're not cut out for real life," Alistair had said when he dropped Ryder back at the Carillon an hour ago. "You're meant to live on the edge. You wouldn't know how to manage a normal existence."

Ryder watched his laundry tumble around in the Whirlpool and wondered if just maybe Alistair had a point.

THE SULLEN TEENAGER on the other side of the deli counter chomped on her gun and tapped her acrylic fingernails impatiently on top of the cash register while Joanna fumbled through her coat pocket for her money.

"I know I have a single somewhere in here," she said with a smile of apology. "It'll just take another moment."

"I don't got all day," the young blonde snapped, barely glancing at Joanna. "There're other people in here, you know."

Joanna went to step out of the way of a man who was waiting to pay for a pack of Camels when the sleeve of her raincoat brushed against the counter and tipped a cup of coffee down the front of her coat.

The counter clerk's sigh of disgust could be heard three states away.

"Do you have some tissues?" Joanna asked. "This is soaking right through."

The clerk rang up the man's cigarettes and said, "In the back behind the soup."

Joanna took a deep breath. "I mean, do you have some you could give me right now?"

"If you want them, you'll have to buy them." She looked through Joanna as if she weren't there.

Joanna turned and stormed out of the store. For the past hour and a half she'd been feeling slightly invisible, but the deli clerk's rudeness was the last straw.

She'd been jostled in the liquor store without so much as an "Excuse me." In the bookstore a woman pushed ahead of her in line as if Joanna's business couldn't possibly be as important as her own. When a man in his sixties called her "ma'am," Joanna had to battle down the urge to kick him in the shins.

It was a compliment to her artistry with makeup that the disguise—improvised as it was—had been so successful, but all she could think about as she let herself into the lobby of the Carillon was the monstrous coffee stain that was spreading across the front of her raincoat.

Great afternoon, she thought as the elevator creaked its way down to the basement. Not only was her self-esteem knocked down a few pegs, but she had left the deli without her quart of milk and now she faced the drudgery of the laundry room.

Perhaps Cynthia had the right idea after all. Maybe growing old gracefully was an outdated notion. Maybe it was better to kick and scream against time, then when all else fails, take a young lover and flee to Greece where they understand the splendors of older women.

The elevator shimmied to a stop and Joanna hurried through the corridor to the laundry room. Greece and a handsome cabana boy certainly beat an evening with a box of Tide and the promise of coffee with Cremora.

She glanced at her watch. Ten to five. At least the laundry room would still be empty and she could wash and dry her coat before the hordes descended upon it later.

The television was on, as it always was, and the end of *The People's Court* echoed through the cavernous room. Joanna slipped out of her coat and was about to pop it into one of the empty washing machines when she heard a low rumble. She turned and her breath caught.

A man of about thirty-five was sprawled in one of those incongruous brightly colored chairs the Carillon's misguided management had strewn throughout the laundry room like overstuffed Easter eggs. His right leg, encased in an art-deco cast, rested on top of a big stack of *People* magazines—with a few *Newsweeks* thrown in for good measure.

His eyes were closed, his arms folded behind his head. His shaggy, disheveled dark brown hair was shot through with reddish highlights and looked as if he'd forgotten to comb it that morning. The low rumble she'd heard was probably an Upper West Side snore.

Joanna tossed her raincoat into the washer and added detergent. Staring at a sleeping man seemed the ultimate invasion of privacy but she couldn't help it. If those chiseled cheekbones and that strong, well-defined jawline of his were any indication, that was one human being who would age beautifully.

Maybe she'd have time to race upstairs, scrub off the makeup and get back to the laundry room before the spin cycle. She reached for her house keys, which rested on top of the washer in a puddle of Dynamo. They slipped from her hand and clattered to the floor.

"Damn," she mumbled, bending down to fish them out from between two bouncing Whirlpools. The keys were just beyond her reach. She got down on her knees, face pressed against one of the machines, red wool cap drooping over her eyes, and pushed her arm farther into the space between the washers.

Five more seconds, she thought. Five more seconds and

she'd beat a hasty retreat to the superintendent's office and beg for help. She'd rather be embarrassed in front of grizzled, grimy Stanley any day than be caught in her sweatpants and kinky makeup by this male Sleeping Beauty who—

"It's not that I don't enjoy the view from here," a male voice said, "but I think you could use a little help."

Let it be Stanley, she thought. Let it be Stanley or the man in 920 with the earrings or the woman in the penthouse with the glandular problem. Let it be Jack the Ripper but please don't let it be the man with the broken leg and a cast straight out of the Museum of Modern Art.

"If you toss me my crutches, I might be able to help you find whatever you're looking for."

Joanna groaned and stood up. She couldn't wait to see his face when he discovered that the view he'd been enjoying belonged to none other than Mother Time.

Chapter Three

The woman with the red wool cap turned around and Ryder almost fell off his chair. He'd never expected that beautiful derriere to belong to a woman so—well, quite so advanced in years. He covered his mouth and coughed in an attempt to mask his surprise.

The woman eyed him warily. "My keys dropped down there." She pointed between the two bouncing baby Whirlpools. "Your arm will never fit."

He was no Arnold Schwarzenegger but she was right. He leaned over and picked up one of his crutches. "Take this. Maybe you can fish them out."

She smiled at him, quite a remarkable smile for a woman well into her golden years. He wondered if it was the result of good genes or brilliant dentistry. Either way, it was irresistible and he smiled back.

"You young men are smarter than I thought," she said, crossing the laundry room in a few long strides.

Ryder laughed. "Resourcefulness isn't the sole property of the over fifty-five set." He handed her the crutch. My God, what incredible eyes she had! They were the vivid bluish-green of the Caribbean on a sunlit day, starred by lashes that—

Get a grip on yourself, man. She's old enough to be your grandmother.

As if on cue, the woman limped slightly as she went back

to the washing machines. *Arthritis,* he thought, watching her. Probably flared up when she least expected it.

A busted leg was a poor excuse for not helping her. He grabbed the other crutch and boosted himself up from his chair.

THE MAN WAS THUMPING his way toward her, and Joanna buried her face between the washing machines as she fished for her house keys.

Don't come too close, she thought as he did just that. All he had to do was see her glossy black hair peeping out of her red wool cap and she'd be lost. The improvised makeup job was adequate for quick glances, but it was hardly professional enough at this stage to withstand scrutiny.

"Maybe I can lift the end of the washing machine and give you more leeway."

He leaned over next to her and Joanna barely suppressed an urge to pull the cap down over her face. Her arm was wedged between the washers and she wiggled the crutch around on the floor until she heard the clink of metal as it hit the keys.

"Success!" She pulled back and drew the keys out with the tip of the crutch. "You're a lifesaver."

She stood up, ready to bolt out the door, when she noticed a funny look in his hazel eyes. No wonder—she was moving faster than a jackrabbit on springs.

You're eighty years old, for heaven's sake. Slow down!

"Our meeting was serendipitous, son," she said, calling upon her one semester of actor's training at Pratt Institute years ago. "I would have had to face Stanley's wrath had it not been for you."

The marvelous-looking stranger tipped an imaginary hat. "My pleasure."

Joanna turned to leave but his hand on her arm stopped her.

"Can I ask you a personal question?"

Oh, God! Here it comes. She nodded; she didn't trust her voice.

"Do you practice yoga?"

She stared at him. "What?"

His lean and angular face reddened. "I've, uh, I've never seen a woman so agile at your—"

Joanna laughed. "At my advanced age?"

"I was trying to find a better way to phrase it."

"Be blunt, my boy," Joanna said, jingling her keys for emphasis. "Say what's on your mind. One of the greatest benefits of old age is the privilege to say what's on your mind."

A roguish twinkle danced in his eyes. "And you're extending that privilege to me, Mrs.—"

"Hayes," she said, pulling her late grandmother's name out of thin air. "Kathryn Hayes. And, yes, I'm extending that privilege."

"Mrs. Hayes," he said, his grin wicked and wonderful, "you have one hell of a great body."

This was getting stranger by the second.

"And you, dear boy, are a charming liar."

"If we bottle your secret, we could make a fortune."

"No secret," Joanna said, edging toward the door. "I smoke, drink and have my way with elderly gentlemen twice a week." That had been the real Kathryn Hayes's personal prescription for longevity.

His laughter was full and hearty. "That's a regimen I can deal with."

She arched an eyebrow. "You fancy elderly gentlemen also?"

"Sorry to disappoint you," he said, his eyes twinkling, "but I'm one of a dying breed."

She made a show of looking him over—something she never would have tried as Joanna Stratton. "A healthy, red-blooded American male," she said. "As I live and breathe..." Wonderful, she thought. Anything less would have been such a waste of manpower.

"You're a sharp woman, Kathryn Hayes," he said. "I like you."

"Old doesn't mean dull, my boy," she said airily. "You remember that."

WITH THAT, Kathryn Hayes disappeared down the corridor in a fragrant cloud of Giorgio before Ryder had time to frame a suitably witty retort. For a full ten seconds he stood balanced on his crutches, trying to figure out exactly what the hell had happened there.

She was the most fascinating, witty and guilelessly charming woman he'd met in months. Hell! In years. The five minutes spent in her company left him elated and energetic and wishing she'd been willing to linger in the laundry room just a little longer.

He couldn't remember the last time a woman had so instantly, totally captivated him. Was it Ingrid in Sweden a few years ago when he was on an extended vacation? Or Pamela in London, whose upper-class witticisms had fascinated him nearly as much as her top-drawer face and form?

The only thing he was sure of was that the woman in question didn't wear heavy-duty support hose or have grandchildren old enough to be his contemporary.

"You need a long rest," he said out loud as he maneuvered back toward his chair to maintain his vigil at the Whirlpool.

A hell of a long rest.

THREE HOURS LATER Rosie Callahan handed Joanna a glass of Campari and soda and sat down opposite her. "You've been staring at me all night, Joanna. Do I have spinach between my teeth?"

"I'm sorry, Rosie." Joanna put the glass down on the dining room table. "I'm thinking of taking on a small assignment and I—" She stopped. How do you tell a statuesque eighty-year-old ex-burlesque star that you're studying her face to understand the patterns of aging?

"You're blushing." Rosie's dark brown eyes glittered. "A complexion like yours is a dead giveaway every time."

"It's hot in here. That damned radiator is like an inferno."

Rosie got up and checked her thermostat. "It's sixty-six degrees and you're a terrible liar."

"Does nothing escape you, Rosie Callahan?" Joanna curled up in the corner of Rosie's big old early American sofa and got comfortable. "I'm thinking of taking on an assignment."

Rosie took a sip of Campari. "I thought you were putting your mascaras in mothballs, as it were."

"That's what I thought, but Benny Ryan made me an offer I can't refuse."

"Great money?"

"Great challenge." She shifted position on the sofa, feeling suddenly awkward.

"Is it a government secret?"

"Hardly that. It's a commercial for a bank. The camera will follow one man as he waits in line for a teller."

"Not terribly interesting, Joanna."

"It spans fifty years."

Rosie laughed into her drink. "Reminds me of Chase when the social security checks come in at the end of the month."

Joanna relaxed. "Now you get the idea. It's up to me to age the character in ten-year increments."

"And that's why you've been staring at me all night."

"Guilty. I apologize if I made you uncomfortable."

"Hell, no, child, you didn't make me uncomfortable at all. I was just afraid my bridgework was slipping and you were too polite to tell me." Rosie leaned forward in her chair. "Look all you want. There's eighty years of living on this face."

Joanna uncoiled herself from the couch and knelt on the floor by Rosie, tilting a lampshade so more light shone on the older woman's face.

"Any nips and tucks?" she asked, touching Rosie's lined cheek with an index finger.

"Not a one," Rosie said. "By the time I left burlesque, I'd carved out a decent niche as a comic actress." Her smile was rueful. "Comic actresses don't need the jawlines of a Roman statuette."

Cosmetic surgery, lightly undertaken, was one of Joanna's pet peeves. She'd seen too many lovely actresses left with permanently anesthetized upper lips or ugly keloid scars where incisions failed to heal properly. That kind of fast-food mentality when it came to beauty both saddened and appalled Joanna.

There was beauty in a face weathered by time as Rosie's had been, a beauty that a surgeon's scalpel could never duplicate. The network of lines surrounding Rosie's deep brown eyes, the permanent smile creases, the furrows in her brow all formed a living history.

"How are you going to do it?" Rosie asked as Joanna noticed the faint pattern of age around Rosie's nose and cheeks. "I don't think Revlon has anything in its bag of tricks to help you."

Joanna resumed her seat on the end of the couch and sipped her Campari. "Do you remember when I did the special makeup on that Grade-Z sci-fi movie a few years ago?"

"The one Cynthia had the bit part in?"

"We used a special latex formula to build the heads for the Venusian mind readers. I think the same formula can help me take a thirty-year-old through the different stages of aging."

"It may not be as easy as you think," Rosie said. "Even now I'm shocked when I look in the mirror and see an old lady looking back out at me. From year to year, the changes are so subtle, you don't even see them."

Joanna thought about Holland and her own mother, Cynthia—two women whose lives revolved around the appearance of the latest gray hair or laugh line. "Some women see it even when it's not happening," she said dryly.

"Aging's not Cynthia's problem," Rosie said. She and Cynthia's mother had been close friends from childhood. "Vanity is. She spends more time with a mirror than any woman has a right to. She's been like that since she was a little girl."

How well Joanna knew. She had grown up mesmerized by her beautiful mother, watching hour after hour as Cynthia studied her reflection in the dressing table mirror and did her utmost to improve upon perfection.

Where other little girls played with Crayolas and finger paints, Joanna had a palette of jewel-tone eye shadows and tubes of lipstick in crimson and vermilion and soft pink for her experiments with color.

Joanna and Rosie talked of Cynthia for a little while, taking bets on how long her romance with Stavros, the Greek god, would last.

"And what about your social life?" Rosie asked, refilling their glasses. "It seems to me you've been spending quite a few nights home alone."

Joanna grinned into her drink. "I'm on a sabbatical, Rosie. I thought you knew that."

"A sabbatical from work, not love. You should be spending your nights dining and dancing, not reminiscing with aging burlesque stars."

Joanna thought about the last man she'd felt even a glimmer of serious attraction toward. "I'm afraid dining and dancing is a far cry from true love. Quite frankly I'd rather spend the evening with you."

"My condolences," Rosie said. "I'd have turned you out on your ear if Bert were in town."

"Rosie!" Joanna's voice registered both amusement and shock. "What about female solidarity? The value of sisterhood? Feminism and all the other—"

"Ah, you youngsters! Didn't anyone ever tell you you can't curl up in bed at night with rhetoric, Joanna?"

The idea of Rosie curling up in bed with the cherubic Bert Higgins made Joanna giggle.

"You're surprised, aren't you?"

"A little," Joanna admitted. "Though, knowing your wicked past, I'm sure I don't know why I would be."

"I haven't told you the half of it, miss."

Joanna had no doubt that the other half would be enough to curl her hair. "Am I old enough to hear it?"

"Probably not. Although if Ryder had shown up tonight, I would have entertained you both with some of the tamer stories."

"Ryder?"

Rosie's face was studiedly bland. "Oh, didn't I tell you? I had invited another guest for dinner."

Joanna sat up straighter. "A male guest?"

"Quite a handsome male, if I do say so."

"What does Bert think about the competition?"

"Bert has no competition. I invited Ryder for you."

"And where did you meet this Ryder person?" Rosie had been known to meet the strangest people in the unlikeliest places. She could be setting Joanna up with the fourth in line at a soup kitchen or the president of Manufacturer's Hanover.

"In the elevator about a month ago. Around the time my winter boots disappeared."

Cynthia had told Joanna about these mysterious disappearances that had been plaguing Rosie the past few months. An occasional waylaid social security check, misplaced groceries, a string of random items missing from her apartment. Rosie added up the facts and claimed harassment. Everyone else— Joanna included—felt the redoubtable Rosie Callahan was beginning to show signs of her age.

Rosie pointed toward her new living room drapes. "He helped me put the cornices up and we became fast friends."

"Is he the Carillon's chief handyman?"

"Lord, no! He moved into the Jensens' old place, 11E with the balcony and the art deco mirrors." Rosie had lived at the Carillon for more than fifty years and was a veritable encyclopedia of Carillon facts and fantasies. "I hear it went for a pretty penny."

That came as no surprise. When the Carillon made the conversion from rental building to co-op, prices had been astronomical. Joanna's mother had taken advantage of the insider's rate and had purchased her own two-bedroom apartment for a price just this side of obscene.

Rose was one of eleven tenants more than sixty-five years old who were protected by city law; they could be forced neither to buy nor to move. Legislation, however, could not protect them from the landlord's wrath. Rosie, the original agitator, had been trying to convince the tenants to band together and demand fair treatment, and in the past few weeks her Coalition of Tenants for a Fair Deal had been growing steadily more vocal.

"Did he know he was being set up with a blind date?"

Rosie gave her a withering glance. "I may be old, Joanna, but I'm no fool. Matchmaking is a delicate art."

Rosie usually had all the finesse of a tractor trailer when it came to affairs of the heart. She probably promised him a combination of Raquel Welch, Linda Evans and Princess Diana and scared the poor man back into his apartment.

"So what does this moneyed stranger do for a living, anyway?" If she knew Rosie, he was probably a lawyer Rosie had wooed over to her cause.

"I have no idea. He seems to stay home a great deal." She told Joanna about the big Rolls-Royce limousine that showed up each morning at ten and the suave English banker type who visited the Carillon's newest resident.

"Maybe it's his doctor," Joanna said, finishing her drink. "Maybe he has a heart problem or something."

"Oh, no," Rosie said. "Ryder is hale and hearty. The only thing wrong with him is a broken leg and that—"

"A broken what?"

Rosie stared at her. "A broken leg."

"Not a broken right leg?"

"Yes, a broken right leg."

Joanna started to laugh. "With elaborate drawings all over the cast?"

"You've met him?"

"Oh, yes, indeed."

"Any fireworks?" Rosie's romantic imagination was in full swing.

Joanna thought about their interlude in the laundry room and the look on his face when she turned around and met his eyes. Her heart might have revved up into double time but she doubted if his had so much as missed a beat. "Afraid not, Rosie."

"I don't understand," Rosie said, shaking her head. "I was certain you two would hit it off right away, being new at the Carillon and all."

Joanna could barely hold in her laughter. "I don't think I'm his type."

"Not his type!" Rosie's small frame swelled with outrage. "Why you're beautiful and bright and—"

"Sorry, Rosie, but I have a feeling Mr. O'Neal likes younger women."

Younger than George Burns, at least.

Rosie was still sputtering about men and their sexual quirks when Joanna said good night. Tomorrow Joanna would explain all about her Kathryn disguise, but for tonight she would let Rosie rant and rave.

Maybe next time Rosie wouldn't be so quick to set up a surprise blind date for Joanna.

And maybe next time the blind date wouldn't be so quick to say no.

Chapter Four

Maybe you had to be in the right mood for it but *Star Wars* wasn't half as exciting as Ryder remembered. Of course, the first times he'd seen it he'd only been with PAX for five years—controlled insanity hadn't yet become second nature to him.

This time the adventures of Luke Skywalker, Han Solo and the beauteous Princess Leia were growing a little dull. With apologies to all, he zapped off the TV with his remote control device and faced the silence of his apartment.

Talk about dull.

Maybe he shouldn't have been quite so eager to say no to Rosie's dinner invitation. Dinner with Rosie was usually a hell of a lot of fun; it had been the prospect of a blind date that put him off.

He'd seen a few specimens from Rosie's eclectic group of friends and knew his dinner companion could be anything from a Playboy bunny nymphet to a woman of Kathryn-Hayes-of-the-laundry-room's more advanced years.

He chuckled and reached for the phone. Actually he'd probably have a better time bantering with Kathryn Hayes than watching a Playboy bunny fumble with the salad fork and try to keep her tail out of the hors d'oeuvres.

"Can I make it in time for dessert?" he asked after Rosie said hello.

"Tired of your own company, are you?"

"You could say that. Even a blind date is better than *Star Wars* for the eighty-seventh time."

"I'm glad Joanna isn't here," Rosie said. "I don't think she'd care for the comparison."

He felt surprisingly disappointed. "Dinner's over?"

"Afraid so."

"What did I miss?"

Rosie described the menu in excruciating detail.

"I don't care about the salad dressing. What does Joanna Stratton look like?"

"Tall and beautiful and too good for a cur like you, Ryder O'Neal. She wasn't thrilled with the idea of a blind date herself. Especially not after meeting you."

"Meeting me? She must have me confused with somebody else."

"How stupid of me." Rosie sounded highly affronted. "I'm sure she meets men with broken right legs all the time."

"Are you sure she met me?" While he wasn't a monk, he wasn't exactly cutting a wide swath through the women of the Upper West Side these days. A tall and beautiful unattached woman was someone he would remember.

He could hear the hesitation in Rosie's voice. "Well, actually she didn't say she met you, but she did describe that Picasso cast of yours to a T."

Now he understood. He and Joanna Stratton had never met. This was just Rosie's way of needling him for refusing her dinner invitation. He decided to play along with her.

"Did you tell her what a great catch I am?"

"No," Rosie said. "I told her you were a spoiled rich kid who rides around in Rolls-Royces with Savile Row Englishmen by day and does God-knows-what by night."

So she'd noticed Alistair and the ubiquitous limousine. It shouldn't come as a surprise; they hadn't been particularly discreet. Yet Ryder had thought limousines were commonplace for the Carillon's gentry.

"That's my uncle," he said, grasping onto the first thought to pop into his head. "He found the apartment for me."

"So you *are* a spoiled rich kid, are you?"

He thought about his ordinary, middle-class upbringing in a frame house on a little street in Omaha, Nebraska, and how far he'd traveled since then.

"Guilty. I've never done an honest day's work in my life." At least, not one he could talk about.

"Why is it I don't know if you're telling the truth or not, Ryder O'Neal?"

He chuckled and changed the subject. "Did you find the keys to your mailbox?" This was the third time in five weeks that Rosie had misplaced something important.

"No, and I've asked Stanley for a duplicate but he says it will take a week. He says I'm getting senile." She paused for a moment. "Maybe he's right."

Bastard, Ryder thought. Forgetfulness sure as hell wasn't the sole province of the elderly. "I'll get a key for you tomorrow, Rosie." A call to Alistair should do the trick. The man's influence was something to behold.

"That's it," Rosie said. "You're a locksmith. I knew I'd figure it out sooner or later."

"Wrong again. I told you I was a spoiled rich kid, didn't I?"

They bantered for a few minutes more about his mysterious occupation, then Ryder stifled a yawn.

"Sorry," he said into the phone. "Life in the fast lane is getting to me."

"It *is* almost ten-thirty," Rosie said dryly. "Maybe you should turn in."

"Good night, Rosie," he said, laughing.

"Good night, old-timer."

He was about to hang up the telephone, happy that he'd been able to deflect her curiosity about Alistair and his occupation when Rosie said, "Ryder?"

"Yes?"

"You got away with changing the subject this time, but don't think you'll always be that lucky."

Click.

Ryder stared at the telephone for a full ten seconds after Rosie hung up on him.

Senile?

Not very likely.

THE NEXT MORNING Joanna woke up early. She washed and dried her hair until it sparkled like spun silk, carefully applied her makeup and slipped into a long-sleeved red minidress and black tights.

The mad urge to do laundry had seized her in the middle of the night. She collected everything marked washable in the apartment and had trekked up and down to the laundry room five times by noon.

Amazing just how much tending those washers and dryers actually needed.

Amazing just how far a woman will go to fool herself.

Finally, around one-fifteen, the only thing left to launder was herself, but the thought of stripping off her clothing and leaping into a top-loading Whirlpool didn't appeal to Joanna in the least.

You might as well face it, she thought as she lugged the spanking-clean shower curtain and guest towels back up to her mother's apartment. *He doesn't spend his time dozing in the laundry room.* That had been a fluke, the same as her visit.

He was probably out right now visiting his orthopedist, trying to describe the wild sexual variation that had broken his leg and landed him in both the *New England Journal of Medicine* and on Dr. Ruth's TV show.

She locked the apartment door behind her and threw the last batch of clean clothes atop the four other batches of clean clothes that were stacked on top of the sofa and the chairs and the credenza.

Holland was still at her audition. Joanna was going to meet her at seven for dinner at The Maltese Falcon, a little cafe on Columbus Avenue, but until then she had an endless expanse of six hours and absolutely no way to fill them.

She was not a woman meant for idleness.

Benny Ryan's job offer could put an end to that idleness, at least for a few days. Yesterday's excursion into the real world in her improvised old-age makeup had gone a long way toward proving to Joanna that she could handle the demands of the job. And her evening with Rosie and the opportunity to really study the patterns of aging had given her new ideas that would help her underplay the obvious and highlight the subtle.

Joanna pulled her enormous leather suitcase from the hall closet and dragged it over to the desk by the window.

The only way she was going to bump into the mysterious stranger with the broken leg and the muscles that went on forever was to coerce Rosie into staging another blind date for them.

Until then, it was back to work.

She opened the suitcase and reached for the heavy-duty Pan Cake #733D, Alabaster Echo.

Some vacation.

"YOU LOOK BORED." Alistair poured himself another gin and tonic from the bar in the back of the Rolls as it cruised up the FDR Drive.

"I am bored."

"I thought lunch in SoHo was the perfect antidote."

"SoHo is boring," Ryder said, feeling like a petulant six-year-old.

Alistair chuckled. "I rather thought you'd like feeding at one of those Yuppie watering holes I hear so much about."

"Did you see the way they were dressed in there? It looked like they'd gotten a group discount from the L. L. Bean catalog." His leather jacket and jeans had been as out of place as a tuxedo at a nudist colony.

Alistair offered him a drink but Ryder shook his head. "I'm glad to see your sardonic humor is returning, my boy. You've been a trifle dour today."

"Not dour. Bored."

"I have the perfect solution for that."

Ryder glared at him. Alistair had been describing that perfect solution all afternoon. "Forget it. I'm not interested."

The chauffeur eased off the FDR Drive and started crosstown toward Columbus Avenue.

"Now I'm the one afflicted with boredom." Alistair's crisp British accent gave each word a certain upper-crust arrogance that often drove Ryder mad. "We need you and you are part of us. It is that simple."

"Nothing's that simple."

Alistair lit one of the foreign cigarettes Ryder hated. "I can see that this taste of civilian life was not one of my better ideas. We should have sent you off to Bali or Tahiti for your R and R."

"You're not afraid I'll be seduced by the lure of the South Seas and end up a beach bum?"

"Somehow I don't fancy you selling coconut oil to tourists, dear boy." Ryder watched as Alistair inhaled deeply on his cigarette. "No, Ryder, where you are concerned, real life's the greatest danger of all."

"How would I know?" Ryder countered. "I've seen damned little of it in the past fifteen years."

Alistair watched him carefully. "My well-honed instincts tell me this is not the most opportune moment, but I'd like to talk to you about a short-term assignment."

Ryder's response was not one found in the handbook.

Alistair pressed on. "The Caribbean is lively this time of year."

Ryder instantly knew he was talking about the crisis at the American embassy on the island of St. George and he wanted no part of it.

"Call Poliakoff or Lewis," he said, grinning as two children in private-school uniforms tried to peek through the smoked-glass windows of the Rolls-Royce as it waited at a red light. "They did a damned good job at the western White House."

"Of course, they did," Alistair said smoothly. "Except that you drew up the diagrams, keyed in the security codes and monitored everything else."

"You weren't supposed to know that." He'd been grooming Ira Poliakoff and Mitch Lewis for bigger and better things. "They can handle anything you throw at them. I was the one who couldn't back off."

"And you think you can now?"

"Yes." He hesitated. "I think I can."

"Pardon me if I find that difficult to believe."

"I don't give a rat's ass what you find difficult to believe, Chambers. I'm damned sick of living out of a suitcase. I want more out of life than an unlimited expense account."

Alistair didn't bother to hide his amusement. "If indeed you are finished, my boy, why do you avail yourself of the organization's largesse?"

Ryder picked up one of his crutches and slammed it twice against the partition between passengers and driver.

"Pull over!" His voice was an angry roar.

The chauffeur, accustomed to abrupt changes in destination and/or passengers, smoothly pulled over and stopped the Rolls.

"It's a long walk, O'Neal," Alistair said as Ryder pressed a series of buttons, then opened the passenger door. "Hardly a delight on crutches."

"I don't give a damn if I have to crawl." Ryder began to maneuver himself out of the plush automobile, awkwardly using the crutches for leverage. "I'm getting the hell out of here now."

"Ah, the impetuosity of youth!" Alistair slid over to the other side and retrieved Ryder's wallet from the floor. "You might need this."

Ryder, who had been inordinately pleased with his grand exit, cursed. "The least you could have done is let me walk a block," he said, accepting the wallet.

"Walk all you want," Alistair said, getting back into the car. "Let off steam. We can talk more about this tomorrow over lunch."

"You can take lunch and stick it up your—"

Alistair laughed and powered the car window up, and Ryder's words fell upon the ears of two Sisters of Mercy, who crossed themselves and offered a quick prayer for his redemption.

The Rolls moved back into traffic. The nuns hurried past. Ryder looked up the street sign and realized he was thirteen blocks away from the Carillon.

Making a point was one thing; being masochistic was something else.

He waited until the Rolls disappeared from view, then stepped into the street to whistle for a cab.

JOANNA WAS INVISIBLE.

That had to be it. Through some bizarre accident of nature she'd been rendered invisible and the reason everyone on Columbus Avenue was shoving past her was because they couldn't see her as she wheeled Rosie's shopping cart back from the grocery store.

What other reason could there be? She wouldn't treat a stray cat the way she'd been treated these past two hours.

Since leaving the Carillon in full septuagenarian makeup and attire, Joanna had been jostled, bumped, cursed at, shoved off the curb, elbowed out of line at the produce scale and generally treated with all the respect reserved for the unwashed destitute of Calcutta.

Correction: The destitute in Calcutta had Mother Teresa to turn to in times of trouble. On the streets of New York, Joanna had no one.

By the time she reached the dry cleaners where she had promised to drop off Rosie's coat, she was having the devil of a time controlling the urge to fling her gray wig into the street, strip off the heavy makeup and challenge the next person who pushed her aside to a duel.

It was a relief to step into Speedy Cleaners and leave the noise and commotion out on the street. She left her shopping cart to the right side of the door and approached the counter, noting with pleasure that Barry was working today. Barry was a starving opera singer who worked in the dry cleaners during the day, sang for his supper as waiter/tenor at Bardolino's in the Village by night and prayed for his big break the rest of the time.

As usual he was poring over *Variety*. He glanced at her, then over at the shopping cart. She wondered if he would recognize her through her disguise.

"You can't leave that thing in here, lady." He looked at her, then back at his paper. "Against the rules."

"It's just for a moment." She kept her voice tremulous and low as she put Rosie's coat down on the counter.

"Rules are rules."

"If I put it outside, someone will steal it." Damn it! She'd just spent the better part of two hours shopping for those groceries and if this arrogant whippersnapper thought he was going to—

"You should have thought of that before."

"If you write up the slip, I'll be gone before you know it."

"If you don't move the cart, I can't write out the slip."

The connection between shopping cart and dry cleaning receipt eluded Joanna. To her intense embarrassment she found herself teetering on the brink of tears.

Joanna Stratton would have leaned over the counter and grabbed Barry by his lemon-yellow tie. Kathryn Hayes didn't have that option; the past two hours had made that fact crystal clear.

"Please just write up the slip," she said, forcing a smile. "You can bend the rules this once."

Barry didn't even look up. "Sorry. Someone might trip and break a leg."

A deep male voice broke in. "I wouldn't worry about that."

Joanna spun around in the direction of the sound and looked up into the gorgeous face of Ryder O'Neal. He wore a pair of faded jeans, a pale blue T-shirt and a slightly ratty leather bomber jacket with enough zippers and pockets to qualify as the genuine article. Even on crutches and with that psychedelic cast on his right leg, he conveyed more deadly power than anyone Joanna had ever seen.

He moved closer.

"Look up when a lady's speaking to you."

Joanna almost laughed as Barry's head jerked up and his beloved *Variety* slid unnoticed to the floor behind the counter.

Barry looked at Ryder for a long moment, then turned toward Joanna. A wide friendly smile spread across his face, the same smile he gave her—unprompted—when she wore her red mini and left her social security card home.

Amazing what a touch of intimidation could do.

"What can I do for you?" Barry's smile widened until Joanna was certain she could perform a root canal job on his wisdom teeth.

She pushed Rosie's coat across the counter. "Cleaned and pressed."

Barry almost clicked his heels. "At your service." He pulled a pencil from behind his ear.

Joanna couldn't resist. She motioned toward the shopping cart. "Even though it's still in here?"

Barry, amazingly enough, didn't miss a beat. "There's an exception to every rule, ma'am. That's what makes horse racing."

Five minutes later Joanna and Ryder were back on Columbus Avenue.

"Two clichés in one sentence," Joanna said, remembering to keep her voice in her newly acquired older register. "The boy has a long way to go."

"The boy's lucky I'm still on crutches," he said as they crossed the street. "I would've flattened him."

"You young people rely too much on physicality," Joanna said, tugging her shopping cart up onto the curb. "Brains are so much more effective than brawn."

Balancing precariously on his crutches, Ryder tried to help her but nearly fell flat on his behind in the process.

"Worry about yourself," Joanna said, touched by his unexpected kindness. "You're the one who's incapacitated."

He stopped in front of a small boutique. "Chivalry isn't totally dead, madam," he said, executing a clumsy bow. "May I have the honor of escorting you home?"

Her heart took an unexpected leap and for a moment she forgot she was seventy-seven-year-old Kathryn Hayes and a flash of fire lit up her eyes.

"You may indeed."

Regal in gray wig and spectacles, Joanna and her shopping cart marched up Columbus Avenue toward the Carillon with a very confused Ryder O'Neal bringing up the rear.

HE WAS in *big* trouble.

Kathryn Hayes had the sexiest walk he'd ever seen in his entire life.

On second thought, maybe that trip to St. George wasn't such a bad idea at that.

Chapter Five

"Kathryn! Slow down!"

For a second the words didn't register. Then Joanna remembered her disguise and the fact that very few seventy-seven-year-old women power-walked while pulling a loaded shopping cart and she stopped abruptly.

My God! she thought as he maneuvered himself through the pedestrian traffic. No man had the right to look that good—or seem that nice. There had to be some flaw somewhere, but she'd be damned if she'd been able to find it yet.

"If you can't keep up with an old woman, you're in sorry shape, my boy," she said as he finally caught up with her. "Maybe you should consider paying Jack LaLanne a visit."

"You're a cruel woman, Kathryn." His smile crinkled the outer corners of his hazel eyes. Joanna had always been partial to men with hazel eyes.

"Not cruel," she said. "Blunt. Maybe you should give up that fancy limousine Rosie told me about and worry about aerobic conditioning."

"Aerobic conditioning?" His laughter mingled with the sounds of the city street. "Now if Rosie Callahan had set you up as my date last night instead of Joanna Somebody-or-other I might have given it a shot."

For the second time Joanna screeched to a halt. Ryder stumbled and just missed falling over the shopping cart.

"Try signaling next time," he said, regaining his balance

on his crutches. "I don't want to trade a broken right leg for a broken left leg."

Joanna ignored him. "That Joanna Somebody-or-other happens to be my granddaughter and I'll have you know she was quite relieved when you didn't show up." What a facile liar she was turning out to be.

"What do you mean, she was quite relieved?"

"Joanna isn't the type of young woman who needs to rely upon blind dates." This whole situation was becoming more ridiculous by the second, but, if she was going to be outrageous, why not go all the way? "Her social calendar is so filled these days, she simply doesn't have time."

They walked another ten feet. This time it was Ryder who stopped.

"She had time to have dinner with Rosie last night."

"And how do you know that, young man?"

"Rosie told me."

"I'm going to have to have to a talk with Rosie," Joanna muttered.

"What was that?"

Terrific. Even his hearing was above average.

"I said, Joanna will have to have a talk with Rosie."

"Why? Was her dinner visit a state secret?"

"No, but I hardly think she'll like her dinner visit being discussed with the man who stood her up." *Cool down,* Joanna thought. *Too much righteous indignation.* Any minute she'd be forced to challenge him to a duel over her own honor.

"And I'm supposed to be happy that she was glad she didn't have to meet me?"

"No happier than she was when you decided a *Star Wars* rerun was preferable to her company."

The look of embarrassment on his face was priceless. "And how in hell do you know about that?"

Joanna smiled. "Rosie."

"I didn't realize you knew Rosie."

"Everyone at the Carillon knows Rosie Callahan."

He probably figured Joanna was part of the Coalition of

Tenants for a Fair Deal that Rosie was trying to get established.

They waited at the corner for the red light to change.

"Do you think your Joanna would give me another chance?" Apparently he had other things on his mind.

Here it was: the perfect moment to reveal her identity, to whip into the nearest telephone booth as Kathryn Hayes and pop out as Joanna Stratton. However, the light changed, the crowd swept them forward and Joanna lost her nerve.

"She's a fair-minded woman," Joanna said. "You should ask her yourself."

"I intend to," Ryder said. "First chance I get."

A blast of wind knocked them back a step and Joanna's gray wig slipped down over her left ear. She tugged it back in place and glanced up at him. One more gust like that and Ryder O'Neal would have his chance sooner than he expected.

IF THERE WAS ONE THING Holland Masters despised, it was being kept waiting. She'd been sitting in the outer lobby of the venerable Carillon Arms for twenty minutes trying to ignore the lascivious looks those two young and scruffy workmen had been aiming at her legs, and cursing Joanna for having the nerve to be out.

No matter that their dinner appointment was for seven and it was only quarter after four—details like that rarely bothered the sometimes imperious Holland.

The doorman ushered an elderly couple with matching mink coats into the lobby, bowing and scraping and nearly licking their boots for a tip. The way he kept his head tucked into his chest, his eyes downcast, the image of obsequious servility—God, that would be perfect for her to use when she auditioned tomorrow for the role of the older daughter in that Off-Off-Off Broadway production.

She closed her eyes and concentrated, committing his movements to memory the same way she did the words in a script.

"Are you all right, miss?"

Who would have expected the doorman to sound so British and so urbane?

"I'm fine." Her concentration wavered. Damn it! She couldn't quite reconstruct the angle of his smile when he pocketed his tip. The left side of his mouth tilted up a little more than—

"I hardly think my concern merits a sneer."

"Would you kindly leave me alone?" She opened her eyes, ready to argue, then promptly wished she could reach out and pull her words back. Standing before her was the most impeccably groomed, perfectly tailored vision of male pulchritude she'd seen in many a moon. She crossed her legs, her best feature, and smiled up at him. "Would you kindly forget I said that?"

"As you wish." He sat down next to her on the marble bench. "My memory is short."

He had that tweedy, outdoorsy smell Holland associated with British suits and unimpeachable pedigrees. His face was tanned and a network of lines surrounded his bright blue eyes. Obviously he was a man who'd lived—and lived well.

"Alistair Chambers," he said, extending his hand.

"Holland Masters."

Alistair Chambers gestured toward the doorman who was fawning over a young model who lived in the building. "Some men should never be given uniforms." His tone was wry and wicked. "Gives them delusions of grandeur."

Holland laughed. "Next thing you know he'll make us march back to Columbus Avenue on our knees."

"He won't let you past security either?"

"I look too untrustworthy." She made a show of looking him over. "You look respectable enough."

"Don't let appearances deceive you, my dear Ms. Masters. I can be a dangerous man."

"Why is it I believe you, Mr. Chambers?"

"You shouldn't." He smiled and she felt it all the way to the soles of his feet. "I'm also an outrageous liar."

"Then we're even," Holland said, struggling to regain her equilibrium before such an onslaught of charm. "So am I."

He reached into the pocket of his Burberry raincoat and pulled out a pack of Player's cigarettes. "Care for one?"

"How wonderful!" She took one and waited while he produced a discreetly elegant silver lighter and touched it to her cigarette. "A man who understands the pleasure of good, old-fashioned vices."

"Ah, yes," Alistair said, inhaling deeply of his own cigarette. "Fine cigarettes, good brandy—"

"Juicy sirloin steaks, baked potatoes with sour cream—"

"A blissful life of indolence and indulgence with words like cholesterol and calories struck forever from our personal lexicon."

The man should be declared an international treasure. "Are all Englishmen as wonderfully decadent as you are, Mr. Chambers?" Maybe she'd been looking for Mr. Right on the wrong side of the Atlantic Ocean.

"But of course," Alistair said, inhaling deeply on his imported cigarette. "Since we lost all of our colonies, we have time to devote ourselves to the more important things in life."

"Such as sitting in the lobby of the Carillon?"

The twinkle in his eyes as his gaze slid appreciatively over her legs made Holland feel as if she were standing in the glow of a warm amber spotlight.

"Such as speaking with you."

Her dialogue coach would be in heaven. "I must say, Mr. Chambers, speaking with you is better than a crash course in Noel Coward."

"You flatter me, Ms. Masters."

Holland's smile widened. "That was my intent."

Alistair glanced at his watch. Holland was quick to note it was a pricey Piaget. "I abhor waiting for people."

Holland glanced at her own trendy and cheap Swatch. "So do I."

He stood up and extended his hand toward Holland. "Perhaps a brandy would ease the pain of waiting."

Holland took his hand and stood up. He was easily five inches taller than she. It was a long time since she'd looked up to a man—in any sense of the phrase. "The piano player at Pat and Mike's is superb."

"Perhaps," Alistair said, as they swept past the two workmen who were repairing the inner door, "but the brandy is pedestrian."

She ran down a list of neighborhood bars and discarded them all. She couldn't imagine this sophisticated British subject trading Yankees baseball stories with the clientele of most of them. "We could go crosstown," she said, praying that something as ludicrous as the pursuit of the perfect brandy wouldn't squelch a beginning as beautiful as this.

She needn't have worried. Alistair Chambers had matters well in hand. "I belong to a private club just a few blocks away," he said as the doorman, eyebrows raised in question, ushered them outside. "If you don't mind walking, they have a Courvoisier second to none."

At that point Holland would have walked to Hoboken and back simply for the pleasure of his company but she was wise enough in the ways of the world to keep that fact private.

"All New Yorkers love walking," she said as they headed toward Columbus Avenue. "It's part of the mystique."

"There's more to the New York mystique than that," Alistair said. "What about this strange predilection for—"

His words trailed off.

"Alistair? Is something wrong?"

He said nothing, just stared up the block. Holland looked and saw nothing unusual, just a man on crutches and an elderly lady pulling a shopping cart. Then she noticed that the elderly lady was wearing white Reeboks with bright red laces, exactly like Joanna's.

"This time she's gone too far."

"I beg your pardon?" Alistair looked down at her.

Holland hadn't realized she'd spoken aloud. "I said, I didn't think she could walk that far."

His interest, however, was instantly piqued. "Do you know that woman?"

"Yes, I do." *But not as well as I thought I did.* "Don't tell me you know her, too?"

Alistair shook his head. "Afraid not. I know the young man on crutches."

"The Carillon?"

"The Carillon."

They stopped walking and waited while the odd couple crossed the street.

"They're having quite an animated conversation, aren't they?" Alistair observed as Joanna and the man approached. "One would wonder what they have in common."

Holland noticed the heightened color of Joanna's cheeks that even five tons of latex makeup couldn't conceal. "Yes," she said, "one certainly would."

And one intended to find out.

JOANNA WAS GIVING Ryder a lecture on dating etiquette, from her vantage point of seventy-seven years, when she noticed an all-too-familiar face.

Holland Masters, looking chic as usual and rather smug, was leaning against the fender of a black BMW. She was in the company of one of the more attractive older men Joanna had seen in a long time. Normally Joanna would have suggested the three of them go out for drinks so she could blatantly pry for information about their relationship.

Not this time. All Holland had to do was say, "See? Your disguise works!" and the possibility of anything developing between Joanna and Ryder O'Neal would go up in flames.

Ignore her, Joanna thought. Walk right by like a perfect stranger. Holland was a smart woman. Surely she'd take the hint.

Holland did take the hint.

Unfortunately, the debonair man with her did not.

"Well, my boy," he said to Ryder, "you seem to have recovered from the snit you were in."

Next to her, Ryder drew in a long breath. The tension between the two men was palpable. "What are you doing here, Chambers?"

The man named Chambers laughed. "Obviously the thing to do is ignore your cordial greeting." He turned toward Joanna. "I'm Alistair Chambers," he said, extending his hand. "And you are—?"

Alistair Chambers was so charming, that Joanna was about to give him her real name when she remembered her disguise. "Kathryn," she said, shaking his hand. "Kathryn Hayes."

"A pleasure, Miss Hayes. I understand that you and Ms. Masters are friends."

Joanna turned to look at Holland. "Good day, my dear," she said, stressing her Kathryn persona. "You're looking well today."

Holland, with classic dramatic timing, kept Joanna waiting for an answer. "So are you, Kathryn," she said finally. "Different, but well."

Joanna glared at her friend. *Say one more word and you're dead.* "Perhaps you should go home and get some sleep, Holland dear. Those late nights seem to be catching up with you."

"You must speak to Joanna about it," Holland said smoothly. "She has this habit of keeping me out late." She turned toward Alistair Chambers. "Her granddaughter is an aficionado of the New York nightlife."

Joanna wanted to hit her over the head with one of Ryder's crutches.

This bit of byplay was lost on Ryder, who apparently had problems of his own. Joanna quickly realized, however, that beneath his cool exterior Alistair Chambers was paying close attention to everything she did. Her awareness of the wig, the heavy makeup, the sound of her voice, all heightened uncomfortably.

"As a matter of fact," Chambers said, his bright blue eyes leveled on Joanna, "Holland and I were in search of the perfect brandy. I don't suppose you and my recalcitrant friend here would care to join us?"

Ryder answered before Joanna had a chance. "Thanks but no thanks. I was just helping Kathryn home."

The fact that Kathryn had pulled her own shopping cart while he hobbled along on crutches was lost on Ryder.

"In that case, we bid you farewell." Alistair's continental charm inched up another notch.

Holland linked her arm through Alistair's. "Don't let Joanna forget about our dinner engagement tonight." Her smile was wicked. "I'm so looking forward to hearing about her new assignment."

"I'll tell her," Joanna said between clenched teeth. "I'm sure she's counting the hours."

Holland and Alistair sailed up Columbus Avenue leaving Joanna and Ryder both off balance.

"What was that all about?" Ryder said as they continued on toward the Carillon. "You two sounded as if you were at each other's throats."

"That's Holland's way. She's been in so many Noel Coward revivals that arch dialogue is second nature to her." She tugged the shopping cart through a particularly nasty pothole. "You and Mr. Chambers didn't seem to be on the best of terms, either. Though I must say, he's a charming devil."

"You're half-right."

"Do I detect a note of sarcasm in your voice?"

Ryder said nothing. Joanna would have let the subject drop; Kathryn didn't have to.

"I take it he's a business associate of yours?"

"Former associate," Ryder grunted.

"And what did you two associate on?"

"Putting out fires."

Both Joanna and Kathryn recognized a closed door when she smacked into one. She turned to safer topics.

"Is he married?"

"Not that I know of." He glanced down at her. "Your friend Holland looks like she can take care of herself." He paused a moment. "Is Joanna like her?"

"Not in the slightest."

"What does she do for a living?"

"She puts out fires."

He grinned. "I deserved that, didn't I?"

Joanna nodded but she felt uncomfortable, as if her clothes had suddenly gotten too tight. "Tell me about your friend Mr. Chambers. If I were thirty years younger, I'd give Holland a run for her money."

Ryder dismissed her question as if Chambers were a waste of time. "He's no friend of mine." He zeroed back in on target. "What color is Joanna's hair?"

"You'd know if you'd gone to dinner last night." *This is getting out of hand,* she thought. *Tell him now. Explain the whole damned thing and be done with it.*

They nodded their way past the doorman and into the inner lobby. Five elderly matrons in their best lunch-at-the-Metropolitan outfits stood chatting near the elevator bank about the terrible attitude of the new help in the Carillon. One of the women held the bright yellow flier Rosie had been distributing about the tenants' coalition.

If Joanna had whipped off her wig right then, she'd have been responsible for five cardiac seizures.

"I have an idea," Ryder said, balancing on his crutches while Joanna pushed the button for an elevator. "Why don't the three of us go out to dinner tonight and—"

"No!" Joanna's voice shattered the genteel stillness of the lobby and brought with it five very well-bred frowns from the Carillon matrons.

"I understand refusing a blind date, but I'm a known quantity now. Why don't you both take a chance, Kathryn?"

She searched for an alibi, then stumbled onto the truth. "Joanna is going out tonight," she said, breathing a sigh of relief. "She and Holland are having dinner."

He was disappointed but not deterred. "Then it's the two of us."

Joanna had to admire a man whose interests went beyond the more obvious divertissements.

"Seven o'clock." That wonderful smile of his was back. "How about the Hard Rock Café?"

For a moment Joanna was sorely tempted but the absurdity of the situation held her in check. "I'll have to ask for a rain check, dear," she said as the elevator door slid open and they stepped inside followed by the matrons, who smelled of Pink Ladies and Chanel No. 5. "I'm not as young as I used to be." She hesitated, the steady stream of nonsense tangling up her tongue. "I...umm...I need more sleep these days."

He stared at her for a long moment and she wondered if the charade had finally fallen apart. "I don't know about that, Kathryn Hayes," he said as the doors slid closed behind them. "Sometimes I think you're the youngest one of us all."

Oh, God, Joanna thought as the elevator bumped its way up to the ninth floor. *You don't know how right you are.*

THE ONLY FOOD left in the apartment was orange marmalade and a stale onion bagel but Ryder was desperate. He'd rattled around from room to room for the past three hours since saying goodbye to Kathryn, half expecting Alistair to show up at his doorstep eager to make another stab at keeping him in PAX.

The man's rhetoric was all too familiar, but the thought of being whisked down to one of those steak places in the West Forties was enough to overcome Ryder's reluctance.

When the telephone rang in the kitchen, he lunged for it.

"You must be anxious for company, O'Neal." Alistair's voice crackled through the phone wire. "Never answer on the first ring. Too obvious."

Ryder leaned against the kitchen counter. "Are you calling to ply me with liquor and fine food?" He could almost taste the steak, medium rare, the outside all dark and crisp and the inside—

Alistair's laugh was amused. "Afraid not. I intend to ply a quite beautiful woman with liquor and fine food."

"Wonderful," Ryder said, staring glumly at the onion bagel and marmalade. "Think of me feasting on bread and water."

"You have my sympathies."

"So why this call, Chambers? Is it just to cheer me up?"

"We need your help."

Ryder groaned. "At least let me get this damned cast off before you start hounding me."

Ryder listened while Alistair explained an emergency on the tiny Caribbean island of St. George where a militant group was holding several Americans hostage on the outskirts of town, protesting U.S. imperialistic domination. They were threatening to blow up the embassy and kill the hostages one by one.

"Tony Alzado is there," Alistair continued, "but he hasn't come up with a way to penetrate the live bombs surrounding the compound."

Ryder fired off three suggestions for ways the live bombs could be rendered harmless, but Alistair had a rebuttal for each of them.

"So what do you want from me?" Ryder asked finally in exasperation. "That's the best I can do over the phone." He wasn't about to tell Alistair of the work he'd been doing toward that very end while recuperating there at the Carillon.

"Exactly why we need you," Alistair said. "The car will pick you up at 0700 and we'll be in St. George before noon."

"I haven't said I'll go."

"You will."

"Not this time, Chambers."

"There's little point in fighting the inevitable, Ryder. I know you too well. Save us both the trouble and say yes now."

The pull was strong, he couldn't deny that, but his ability to resist was surprisingly stronger. Ryder hung up the telephone without another word, but the victory was Pyrrhic. He knew Alistair would call back and, when he did, Ryder would give in.

For the first time since his accident, he realized that he might never be able to break away, that he'd waited too long to have it all.

The work had been part of his life since he was a callow, nineteen-year-old airman first class in Omaha, Nebraska, a kid with a shortage of book learning but an unbelievable grasp of electronic principles beyond the reach of men with Ph.D.'s after their names. They'd sat him down to evaluate his cryptographic communications skills and he'd scored right off the chart the first time he set eyes on the equipment.

Immediately, he was lifted from the ranks of the ordinary and moved to an organization so secret that few outside the highest echelons of government were aware of its existence. Before he was twenty-five, Ryder had worked on protection devices for aircraft in the Vietnam war, reconnaissance equipment to monitor the proliferation of Soviet weapons in Afghanistan and, most important, bomb-detection apparatus meant to protect U.S. embassies abroad.

Right now he had the highest security clearance given to a civilian not in military work, more money than time in which to spend it and a vast and growing loneliness that work—no matter how important, how necessary—could never fill.

Once before he'd had the chance to sample life in the mainstream. He'd been working in London on some high-tech security equipment for members of the British Parliament when Valerie Parker, daughter of a member of the House of Lords, came into his life and treated him as if he were the pot of gold at the end of the rainbow.

She was young and idealistic, the product of the finest schools and most genteel upbringing the British Isles had to offer. She was only four years younger than he, but Ryder felt centuries older. Idealism, innocence such as hers were traits that had long ago disappeared from his character.

When she offered herself to him, heart and body, he took and took again and never bothered to consider the true value of the gift until the day he left for a new assignment in Taiwan.

Valerie had burst into tears before he finished breaking the news to her. "But I love you, Ryder," she said, her sobs making her difficult to understand. "I want to be with you forever."

He'd gently removed her slender arms from around his neck, her words feeding his male ego.

"Nothing's forever, Val," he said, smoothing her blond hair away from her cheek. "You knew that when this started."

But, of course, she hadn't known that. How could she when her heart was telling her forever was within their grasp? He'd been so accustomed to the cool blondes whose bodies refreshed him like a gin and tonic on a summer day, to women whose approach to sex was as uncomplicated as his, that he didn't recognize Valerie's pain even when it stared him in the eye.

His father's legacy to him.

It wasn't until he was halfway to China and he received a cable telling him that she'd washed down a handful of Seconal with a bottle of her father's Dom Perignon that he understood exactly what he'd done.

The parallel between Valerie's pain and his own mother's wasn't lost on him.

Fortunately, however, Valerie Parker was blessed with the resiliency of youth. Her pride had been wounded but not her spirit. She came back from heartbreak, and a few years later married the son of a British diplomat who gave her what Ryder could not: commitment.

The experience changed Ryder. From that time on, he approached his work with a zeal bordering on obsession, willing to disappear within PAX and put his own life and future on hold. For all his grandiose attempts at saving the world, he'd done one hell of a lousy job when it came to saving one person. He'd managed to convince himself he wasn't like everyone else—he didn't need love; he didn't want commitment.

What he had was all that he wanted.

But these weeks as a civilian had changed him. The visit to his family had pointed out the empty spaces in his life. Holding his newest niece in his arms, he had felt a stab of envy for all he was missing, all he'd cavalierly cast aside when he was too young to know better.

He was sick of being needed only when the specter of death

hovered nearby, tired of dealing in abstracts, hiding behind security clearances and clandestine missions, with no one but Alistair to talk to.

He opened the jar of marmalade and spread some onto the stale bagel.

Maybe that was why Kathryn Hayes was such a revelation to him. Because of the nature of his profession, his relationships with women—except for Valerie—had been mutually pleasurable but fleeting. He had to rely on whatever charm and looks he had at his disposal because more serious, meaningful communication was impossible.

Kathryn wasn't interested in his money or his looks or his bed. She said what she thought, and said it with a vengeance, and Ryder found himself enjoying this taste of reality more than he'd imagined possible. A broken leg had been a small price to pay for opening his eyes to the possibilities beyond PAX.

The combination of onion bagel and orange marmalade was disgusting beyond description. He swept the whole mess into the garbage and, grabbing his crutches and his jacket from the hall closet, set out to find dinner and, if he was lucky, some companionship.

And, if he was very lucky, maybe he wouldn't spend the night alone.

Chapter Six

Joanna was too lazy to go out to dinner by herself, so after she washed off the heavy makeup she changed into a night-gown, she settled in front of the VCR with a Lean Cuisine, a bottle of Soave and *The Big Chill* for company, fully prepared to feel sorry for herself.

Kevin Kline, however, proved to be a wonderful antidote for self-pity, and she was just musing on the definite resemblance between the actor and the mysterious Ryder O'Neal when she heard a crash from Rosie's apartment next door, followed by a yelp that sent chills up Joanna's spine.

She untangled herself from the mountain of magazines on the couch and tapped on the wall between her mother's apartment and Rosie's.

"Rosie! Are you all right in there?"

No answer, just the sound of things being tossed on the floor.

She pounded the wall again. "Rosie! What's going on?"

Rosie's voice, muffled and indistinct, floated through the wall followed by the sound of another, very male voice. Joanna's heart thudded against her breastbone. She knew Bert's lilting Irish voice and that very definitely was not it.

Barefoot, Joanna raced out of her apartment and brought her fist down hard on Rosie's door.

"Come on, Rosie! Answer the—"

The door swung open and Joanna found herself staring up into the very amused eyes of one Ryder O'Neal.

"What in hell is going on? Where's Rosie?" Her heart thumped madly with terror but her terror took an abrupt turn into shock when Ryder started to laugh. "What's going on?"

"You'll never believe it."

She wasn't in the mood for riddles. "If you don't tell me where Rosie is by the time I count to three, I'm going to call the police."

He ushered her into the hall and closed the apartment door. "Rosie's in the bedroom counting her girdles."

Joanna's temper exploded. "That does it!" She reached for the phone at the end table. "I'm calling the cops right now."

Ryder sat down on the monstrous couch that had seen better decades and put his good leg up on the coffee table. "You'll feel pretty foolish when they find Rosie up to her elbows in Maidenforms."

Joanna bent down and pushed his unbroken leg off the tabletop. "That's an antique," she snapped, "not a footstool."

"Put the phone down," Ryder said, "and I'll pretend you didn't do that."

Another crash came from the rear of the apartment. Joanna slammed down the phone and ran for the back bedroom where she found Rosie, unbelievably, surrounded by a spandex and Lycra mountain. The older woman was making separate stacks of the panty girdles, the all-in-one foundation garments and the long lines, carefully noting each one in a green steno pad.

Joanna heard the thump-thump of Ryder's crutches as he came up behind her.

"Do I hear an apology?"

She ignored him and walked over to Rosie. "Rosie, are you all right?"

Rosie nodded and continued sifting through the stack of girdles.

Joanna glanced around in shock. Housecoats and slippers and stockings lay scattered on the floor. A jewelry box rested upended by the radiator. The contents of three bureau drawers had been emptied on the club chair near the window. Scarves and gloves and winter caps were piled on the sill and atop the portable TV in the corner.

"Rosemary Agnes Callahan, if you don't tell me what's going on—"

"Shh." Rosie swatted at Joanna as if she were a pesky housefly. "Let me finish counting the panty girdles."

The whole world was going insane. Joanna picked up one of the bed pillows, covered her mouth with it and let out a shriek of frustration.

"If you're through having a tantrum, I can explain everything."

She turned toward Ryder, who was balanced in the doorway on his crutches. "I wish someone would."

It turned out Ryder had gone out for dinner and, when he came home, he bumped into Rosie in the lobby.

"She'd gone to see a Greta Garbo revival at the Thalia—"

"Not Greta Garbo," Rosie corrected, looking up from her steno pad. "Greer Garson. *Mrs. Miniver*, to be exact."

Ryder grinned. "Greer Garson. She invited me up for a drink, and as soon as we got inside the door, Rosie knew something was wrong."

Joanna looked at the disaster Rosie's once-immaculate bedroom had become. "I should say so."

"She knew before she even saw the bedroom," Ryder said. "Everything looked the same to me, but she walked straight in here, opened her dresser drawer and said Stanley had been in here."

"I've heard a few stories about Stanley," Joanna said carefully, "but I don't think he'd search someone's apartment."

"Search, nothing," Rosie said, sticking her pencil behind her ear. "He stole three of my favorite girdles."

Joanna laughed out loud. "Come on, Rosie! That's absurd."

"I'm telling you he did and it's the second time. Two weeks ago he took my best Bauer & Black support hose, the good ones with the elastic tops."

Joanna looked over at Ryder, who was now leaning against the doorjamb. She shrugged. She looked back at Rosie.

"I really don't think Stanley would steal your underwear, Rosie." She started to chuckle despite herself. "Wouldn't it be easier to go over to Macy's and buy his own girdle?"

"Don't get smart with me, miss," Rosie snapped back. "This is the *Gaslight* treatment he's giving me." She started counting her long-line bras.

"*Gaslight?*"

"An old Charles Boyer-Ingrid Bergman movie," Ryder explained. "The ne'er-do-well husband tries to convince the naive young wife that she's going insane."

With her film and theater background, Joanna was embarrassed that the reference had eluded her. "Why would Stanley want to do something like that?"

Rosie snorted in disgust. "You're a babe in the woods, Joanna. Money."

"There's a black market in used Maidenforms?" Rosie really was losing her grip on reality.

Rosie refused to dignify Joanna's question with an answer and continued her sorting.

Ryder answered instead. "Selling apartments is big business, and Rosie stands in the way of someone turning a tidy profit."

Joanna made a face. "There are only nine unsold apartments in the Carillon," she said, remembering a notice she'd seen posted in the laundry room. "I find it difficult to believe the management is in any fiscal pain." Certainly not if the horrendous amount Cynthia had paid for her own piece of the venerable old building were any indication.

"You *are* naive," he said, moving into the bedroom. "What you can't have is always more appealing than what you can. It's human nature."

"Corporations aren't human," Joanna pointed out, suddenly conscious of his extremely male presence in the small bedroom and of the fact that she was standing there in a sheer nightgown. If Rosie's bed hadn't been littered with enough lingerie to stock Macy's basement, she would have wrapped herself in a chenille bedspread and sprinted for the door; instead, her only choice was to brazen it out.

"The people who run the corporations are," he answered, "and therein rests the problem."

This was a cynical side of him she hadn't seen that afternoon, and it threw her off balance. She turned away from him and said good-night to Rosie, who had just discovered three more pairs of support hose were missing. She started to do a recount of her full slips.

Joanna turned for the door, only to find Ryder blocking her exit.

"You're pretty agile on those things," she said, motioning toward the crutches.

"When I need to be." The smile was the same one he'd given her as Kathryn, but this time it was laced with undercurrents that were unmistakably sexual.

"Don't look at me like that," Joanna said, aware of the flimsy nightgown she wore and the bright light at her back. "I feel foolish enough as it is."

"Let me see you to your door. That's not exactly the right outfit for strolling the halls at midnight."

"I won't be strolling the halls," she said. "I live next door."

"Next door? I thought that was Kathryn Hayes's apartment."

"It is. I'm her granddaughter." She found herself perpetuating the ruse before she had a chance to think straight.

His eyes widened. "Joanna of the blind date?"

Her smile spread slowly as she relished his shock. "One and the same."

"If Rosie had told me you were this beautiful, I might have considered it."

"How flattering," Joanna drawled, "but it wouldn't have made any difference. I don't accept blind dates."

"Not even if they've been screened by your friend and your grandmother?"

"Not even if they come with a four-star rating from Man-watchers International and a security clearance from the Pentagon."

"Of course, now that you know me, I no longer qualify as a blind date."

"We haven't even been introduced."

He snapped his fingers. "Semantics. I'm Ryder O'Neal. You're Joanna Stratton. Let's have dinner tomorrow night. We can even invite Kathryn."

Rosie looked up, her brown eyes questioning. "But Kathryn—"

Joanna enveloped the woman in a bear hug. "Don't ask questions, Rosie," she whispered in her ear. "I'll explain it all tomorrow."

Not one to press her luck, Joanna headed through the hall toward the front door of the apartment, followed by Rosie and Ryder. Rosie was ranting about Stanley and retribution, and Ryder sounded a bit distracted. Joanna had a pretty good idea what was distracting him. Whatever happened to flannel long johns and respectable bathrobes, anyway? God only knew what was visible through her nightgown.

She paused at the door while Rosie unlocked it.

"Make sure both Medeco locks are bolted after we leave," Ryder warned Rosie, "and secure the windows the way I showed you."

"Such a worrier." Joanna had never heard Rosie's voice so soft and affectionate—not even with Bert Higgins. The woman looked up at Joanna. "You best lock up, too. If Stanley sees those frillies of yours that I saw in the laundry room, he'll be in his glory."

With a wicked wink, Rosie closed the door on the two of them and Joanna heard the rapid click-click of the locks being bolted.

Joanna was having a terrible time regaining her composure and the presence of Ryder O'Neal was largely responsible. He followed her the ten feet to her own front door.

"Care to tell me about those frillies Rosie mentioned?"

The look she gave him would have stopped a more cautious man. "Thanks for seeing me home," she said, unlocking the door. "Good night."

"Aren't you going to invite me in for a nightcap?"

"I hadn't planned on it." She shielded her body behind the partially opened door. "How about a rain check?"

His grin was boyish and undeniably effective—even more so now that she wasn't in septuagenarian makeup. "I always say there's no time like the present."

Joanna hesitated. It was close to midnight. Inviting a stranger, no matter how attractive, into her home could be risky.

She considered the prospect of drinking Soave alone by the light of the VCR, then looked down at the big, bulky cast on his leg. How dangerous could he be? Even Rosie could outrun him. "Listen, I want to change my clothes. Why don't you come back in five minutes?"

His grin slid from boyish to dangerously sexy. "Don't change on my account."

"I'm not," Joanna said. "I'm changing on *my* account."

If she were smart she'd get out the gray wig again. Kathryn could handle the situation. Joanna wasn't altogether sure that she could.

ALISTAIR USUALLY had trouble sleeping the night before a big assignment and, despite the way he'd downplayed it to Ryder, the trip to St. George island *was* a big assignment.

He had taken the beauteous Ms. Masters to Le Cirque and they had quite frankly delighted each other. There were three things in the world that Alistair adored: beautiful women, good conversation and fine food. All three were in evidence that evening.

If there hadn't been so many last-minute details to attend to before flying out in the morning, he would have suggested a room at the Plaza with a view of Central Park, a wide soft bed and a magnum of champagne beside it, but duty called.

Besides, Ms. Masters was not a woman made for halfway measures and he was not a man to deny himself full pleasure.

When it happened—and it *would* happen, they both knew that—he wanted the luxury of time to enjoy her.

And so he was back in his PAX-provided apartment on Fifth Avenue, alone except for his brandy and pipe and computer. Using the access numbers that changed daily, he'd brought up all the necessary information on tomorrow's assignment and printed it out, encoded of course, for Ryder.

He had no doubts whatever that O'Neal would take on the assignment.

In fact, if Alistair knew Ryder as well as he thought he did, O'Neal would have the solution worked out before the plane landed, and then have half of the intricate electronic equipment wired before the limousine got them to the compound where they'd be working.

There was absolutely no need whatever for the nagging, uneasy feeling that nipped at him and made him feel as if he'd forgotten something vital to the assignment.

Quickly he tapped in the codes and watched as more and more information filled the screen. The situation was holding steady. The travel arrangements were confirmed. Even the weather was cooperating.

Nevertheless the uneasy feeling remained.

Alistair was about to get up and pour himself another brandy when he noticed the dusting of age spots clustered near the knuckles of his right hand. He'd had them for at least ten years now. They were unsightly, yes, but unavoidable. Part and parcel of the inevitable aging process.

He'd watched cohorts—both men and women—fight age with drugs and scalpel but, short of wearing gloves, no one had managed a way to hide this telltale sign. How many times had he been introduced to a dazzling movie star with the taut jawline of a teenager, only to have the illusion unmasked literally by her own hands.

Something was beginning to come to him, an observation pushed to the back of his mind in the rush of the day's events.

He closed his eyes and called up the memory the way he called up information on his screen.

Ryder and that elderly friend of Holland's, Kathryn Hayes. Slightly stooped posture. Clear blue-green eyes. Hair of gun-metal-gray. Face a network of wrinkles and lines.

Her hands.

Her hands were smooth and pale, the nails perfect, translucent ovals. No liver spots, no unsightly veins, no arthritic swelling around the knuckles. They were the hands of a much younger woman.

He punched in yet another code, typed in the words, "Kathryn Hayes, Carillon Arms, New York City," then sat back.

He didn't have long to wait. The screen flashed "No Information Available."

Impossible. The only people without information were either illegal aliens or undercover agents, and even then it was usually just a matter of expending a bit more effort before he came up with something. Ryder O'Neal was one of the few men whose identities were shielded by all the diplomatic and bureaucratic secrecy the international agency could manage.

Alistair switched to the D Code for classified information, typed in the woman's name, the full street address, and Manhattan, instead of the catch-all New York City, which encompassed all five boroughs. If he'd known her phone number and zip code, he would have added them for good measure.

He pushed the Enter key and waited.

Again the No Information Available code.

Alistair's metabolism made the shift into overdrive as his adrenaline soared the way it always did when he came face-to-face with the unexpected.

His fingers flew across the keypad as he entered in the complicated, ever-changing series of identification codes and access information that booted him up into the Top Secret, Code L file.

A Kathryn Hayes had once lived in the Carillon Arms in an apartment owned by one Cynthia Hayes del Portago, but no longer.

Kathryn Hayes died in 1981.

Someone was taking her place.

RYDER LET HIMSELF into his apartment and tossed his jacket over the back of a chair. The image of Joanna Stratton in her sheer nightgown made it difficult for him to think straight.

At lunch he'd been concerned only with making the stubborn Englishman understand that it was time for him to break free from PAX and the obsession with man's capacity for destruction and to start concerning himself with his own future.

For fifteen years Ryder had willingly let himself be swept into a secret world that existed parallel to the world in which most people lived. The world Alistair had opened up to him so long ago was more violent, more exciting, more dangerous and ultimately more fulfilling than anything he'd imagined in his wildest James Bond fantasies.

But, in that moment when he first saw Joanna on Rosie's doorstep, he finally understood Alistair's words.

Real life was more dangerous.

When Alistair said that to him earlier that afternoon, Ryder had yet to meet Joanna Stratton. He had yet to feel his heart tumble inside his chest as he looked into her blue-green eyes. He had yet to understand exactly what it was Valerie Parker had felt when she fell in love with him.

Fifteen years of training to follow his gut instincts told him that this dark-haired woman was more dangerous to him than anything on earth.

And nothing in his training gave him the slightest clue on how to protect himself even if he wanted to.

JOANNA'S FINGERS SHOOK as she buttoned the last button on her silk shirt and looked at herself in the mirror. Thank God she didn't look as nervous as she was feeling.

Any moment Ryder O'Neal would ring her doorbell and she'd let him into the apartment and tell him the truth.

"I'm a makeup artist," she said to her reflection. "I was practicing a technique for a job I have next week."

She'd say she was sorry to have pulled him into the middle of it, to have made him grow fond of a woman who no longer existed, but things just got out of hand. He didn't have all those laugh lines around his eyes for nothing. He was bound to see the humor in it.

But whether or not he saw the humor, the ruse was over. Juggling identities was too wearing on her nerves. Besides, when he looked at her in her nightgown, the feelings he inspired were definitely not Kathryn's.

So when the doorbell rang, Joanna went to answer it, feeling jumpy but certain that what she was about to do was the right and proper course of action.

Ryder was minus his crutches. With his right hand he gripped an ivory-handled cane, with his left he held up a bottle of Ruffino. For some reason he seemed bigger than she remembered, more male, more sexually demanding.

"Hi." A smile hovered at the edges of his mouth. "Can I come in?"

Joanna felt as if she were surfacing from a deep and dreamless sleep. She stepped aside and as he maneuvered past her, cane tapping loudly against the parquet floor, she caught the scent of his skin and her heart tumbled against her ribs.

There had been men in the years since she lost Eddie, but none who came close to making her feel quite this open, quite this vulnerable. It seemed a thousand years since she had walked down that aisle with her head filled with dreams that never came true. Only her fierce determination had kept her going; only her unshakable inner strength had kept her sane.

And now the same woman who had prided herself on her strength, felt as if she were standing in the eye of a storm with no shelter within reach. No safe place to hide.

She closed the door, took a deep breath, then turned to face him.

"We'll have to be quiet," she said finally as he lowered himself onto the couch. "Kathryn's in the next room and I'd hate to wake her up."

Maybe the storm would safely pass her by.

Chapter Seven

Inviting him inside was her first mistake.

Joanna watched as Ryder filled their glasses with Ruffino. The sleeves on his cream-colored sweater were pushed up past his elbows and her eyes were drawn again and again to the muscles of his forearms with their pattern of deep blue veins.

After years of working closely with some of the most handsome and charismatic men in the world, Joanna had thought herself immune to the charms of a mere mortal.

That was her second mistake.

Somehow when she was hidden away in her Kathryn disguise, she hadn't been fully aware of his magnetism. Certainly she had noticed the handsome face and appreciated the lean, tough body but somehow he had seemed more boyish, more malleable than he seemed now as he sat in the living room.

There was nothing boyish about him, nothing malleable or soft. That sparkle in his hazel eyes covered pure steel. Had her disguise somehow dimmed her perceptions or had she merely seen what she wanted to see and disregarded everything else?

He handed her her glass and held his own aloft.

"To Rosie," he said, clicking his glass against hers, "and her missing Maidenform. I'm in her debt."

Joanna smiled but said nothing. She didn't trust her voice. As Kathryn she had been won over by his kindness. As herself, she was overpowered by his sexuality.

There was something in the air between them, something so electric that her scalp tingled from it, making her want to throw caution to the winds and tell him everything. But there was something to be said for an imaginary grandmother asleep in the next room.

The urge to melt against him, to feel his lips on hers was so powerful that only the strength of her own lie kept Joanna in her seat.

She took a sip of wine, acutely aware of her lips against the rim of the glass, of the burst of flavor against her tongue, the warmth that trickled down her throat and into her stomach. Even the feel of the fragile stem of crystal between her fingers was heightened, turned into something sensual by the simple fact that he was watching her.

He knows what I'm thinking. The look in his eyes was so blatantly sexual that there was no doubt in her mind. Solitary, strong Joanna Stratton—the woman many men wooed but few had ever won—had finally met her match.

She took another sip of wine and cleared her throat. "So, tell me," she said, leaning back in her chair, "how long have you known Rosie?"

His gaze never wavered. "Not too long."

"Three days? Three months? Three years?"

"About three weeks. We met on the elevator. She was going to search through Stanley's garbage for her missing curtains."

Rosie's exploits were getting more and more bizarre. "Stanley isn't a man to cross, Ryder. Not if you value little things like heat and hot water. I hope you didn't encourage her."

"I didn't encourage her," he said with a smile. "I helped her look."

"You may find Rosie amusing," Joanna snapped, "but her situation isn't amusing at all. These flights of fancy are going to find her without a home."

"I thought the New York City housing laws protected her."

"Not if she's declared a public nuisance or her apartment's

deemed a safety hazard. If Stanley caught her sifting through his trash, he could even have her arrested.''

"Back up a little," Ryder said. He didn't appear to be properly chastened. "What do you mean, 'flights of fancy'?''

Joanna took another sip of wine. "That should be obvious. Certainly you don't believe Stanley, or anyone else for that matter, is sneaking into her apartment to steal kitchen curtains and Maidenform bras.''

"Not bras," he said. "Girdles.''

Joanna ignored him. "You may find the situation amusing, but I don't. Rosie's imagination could put her out on the street.''

He polished off his wine and set the empty glass down on the tabletop. "Maybe it's not her imagination.''

"Don't tell me she has you suspecting foul play.''

"You've met Stanley," Ryder said. "Would it surprise you?''

"I admit Stanley has his hand out all the time," she said, "but that doesn't make him guilty of harassment. Besides, he doesn't own the building. What would he gain from evicting her?''

"Come on, Joanna. No one is that naive. Who pays his salary?''

His point was a good one, but the situation seemed too implausible for Joanna to take seriously. "I've known Rosie for many years," she said, "and she is getting a tad forgetful. Is it so unlikely that she's misplacing a few things?''

Ryder leaned forward. "A misplaced blender?''

"Don't tell me her blender is missing, too.''

"And her electric wok. Do you still think it's senility or are you willing to admit something might be going on?''

"She probably rearranged her cabinets or gave the wok to Goodwill. She *is* almost eighty years old, Ryder.''

"So is Kathryn," he shot back, "but she's sharper than most thirty-year-olds I know.''

There's a good reason for that, Joanna thought as she finished her wine.

"You need a refill."

Joanna looked up at the sound of his voice. Suddenly she was aware of nothing save the warm sound of his words, the cool sleek feel of crystal beneath her fingers, the intense, almost erotic silence of the darkened room. Joanna's heart pounded in her ears like the sound of the ocean after a storm. The moment seemed to wrap itself around the two of them, drawing them closer, urging them toward the unknown.

The invitation was in his eyes, in the way his gaze lingered softly on her mouth and trailed down her throat. It was there in the touch of his hand as he reached toward her, in the way he leaned close enough for her to sense the desire building inside him.

How simple it would be to join him on the couch, to give in to this insane fever that burned deep inside the pit of her stomach and flared outward.

And she knew exactly how it would be....

Joanna would remove her clothes slowly, fingers trembling, letting her shirt slide to the floor along with her slacks in a puddle of silk. There would be something savagely exciting in exposing herself to this man, in watching the effect her beauty would have on him.

Ryder's hands, large and strong, would reach out to cup her but she would elude him, letting her hands drift across her stomach and thighs, making him wonder how she would feel against him. The air in the apartment was chilly and her nipples would grow hard and tight, dark against the paleness of her skin, and he would once again reach out for her as she lifted her hair off the back of her neck and—

"Joanna? I said, do you want some more wine?"

She blinked and noticed she was sitting, fully clothed, in the club chair while Ryder waited for her to answer.

"Yes," she finally managed. "Make it a double."

IT WAS A GOOD THING he'd broken his leg because if it weren't for that bulky cast, Ryder would have been tempted to sweep

Joanna off her feet and up to his apartment where he could make love to her all night long.

In her lacy nightgown she had raised his temperature a few degrees; but now, just sitting there in pants and a simple shirt she was turning his entire body to molten steel.

He'd never seen such pure desire in a woman's eyes before. Hell, if he looked in the mirror he'd probably see the same look in his own.

He wanted to slide his hands into those black silk pants of hers and cup her buttocks, feel the soft flesh of her hips, slide his fingers to the top of her thighs and beyond, but as much as he wanted her, naked and writhing beneath him, some gut instinct held him back. Oh, there were ways around the inconvenience of a cast—he'd already explored two or three of them a few weeks ago. Pleasure was where you found it, and pleasure was something he knew all about.

But this went beyond pleasure.

If he and Joanna Stratton were to act out the fantasies that charged the air between them with fire and dreams, there would be no turning back. He would want everything she was. He would want to own her, heart and soul, to slip inside her mind and know her secret thoughts, her wildest dreams.

It was the last thing on earth that he was ready for.

He refilled her wineglass and handed it to her.

"Has Kathryn had any trouble with Stanley?" he asked.

Joanna shook her head. "None at all," she said, taking a sip of wine. "It's not her apartment."

"Yours?"

A drop of wine lingered on her bottom lip and he longed to touch his tongue to it and savor the mingled sweetness of her breath and the wine. The tip of her own tongue darted out to catch it and his entire body responded to the artless eroticism of the act.

"My mother's." Her eyes lingered on his as if she knew what he'd been thinking.

"So that explains the name on the doorbell."

"You're very observant."

"It's part of the job."

"Which is?"

Damn it to hell. In just a few weeks of inactivity, he'd grown dangerously careless. Even if he managed to break free of the organization, a slip like that could cost innocent people their lives.

"Nonexistent." He grabbed onto the first idea that presented itself. "I'm part of the idle rich."

"Lucky you." She seemed to accept it.

"How do you keep body and soul together, Joanna Stratton?"

"I'm a makeup artist."

"Avon or Mary Kay?"

She laughed. "Neither one. I do films, some stage and a lot of still photography."

"Interesting work?"

"Oh, yes," she said. "Not to mention socially relevant."

"I imagine keeping Redford beautiful for his public is serious business."

The soft lines of her dazzling face sharpened. "Care for me to make a few observations on the idle rich?"

"Entertainment is necessary for the soul. I didn't mean it as an insult, Joanna."

She sipped her wine. "I know you didn't. I'm going through a midlife career crisis at the moment and I guess I'm feeling hypersensitive."

"Aren't you a bit young for a midlife crisis?" She couldn't be more than twenty-seven or twenty-eight.

"I'm thirty-two," she said, "but I've been working since I was twenty." She shook her head in bemusement. "Can you imagine? Twelve years of worrying if the mascara is going to smudge or the foundation is properly blended. My epitaph will probably read, 'Joanna Stratton: She really knew her eye shadows.'"

"So why don't you change fields?"

She looked at him as if he'd sprouted a second head. "Easy for a member of the idle rich to say. This is my one and only talent and since I'm my sole support..." She let her words trail off and his curiosity heightened.

"You've never been married?"

"Once," she said quietly. "A thousand years ago."

A tactful change of subject was in order but tact had never been his strong suit. "Divorced?"

"That's none of your business, Ryder."

"You're not still married, are you?" He hadn't always been an example of moral rectitude but consorting with married women was strictly off-limits.

Joanna stood up and put her wineglass on the table. Her silk shirt was loose and flowing and he caught a tantalizing glimpse of bare skin.

"Eddie died in a crash in 1973," she said, her voice flat and emotionless. "I thought he was on his way to Kadena Air Force Base in Okinawa. He was really going to Texas to see the woman who was about to have his child."

She turned toward the window, her back straight and proud, and memories he'd tried to keep at bay since Valerie rushed in at him. He'd forgotten how easily a heart could break.

Let her go, he thought as he memorized the sweet curve of her waist, the sleek line of her legs. *If you remember anything about real life, let this woman go.*

She needed a man who went to work at nine and came home at six, a man whose world revolved around her, a man to sleep beside and raise a family with, a man whose tomorrows would be the same as his today.

She didn't need a man whose life had revolved on the axis of self, a man who owed so much to so many and had so little chance of finding his way back to the real world.

What Joanna needed wasn't his to give, and until he broke free of PAX any promises he made to her would be promises written in sand.

She deserved better.

And, unfortunately, so did he.

THE WORDS ECHOED in Joanna's head. No one, not even her mother or Holland, knew the entire truth about the tragic end

of her marriage to Eddie Carr. She'd adopted the stance of the
grief-stricken widow, while inside her, anger tore at her heart
and eroded her self-esteem.

And now tonight, to this virtual stranger, Joanna had vom-
ited up the words that had rested like bile in her throat for so
long. She would have given anything to pull those ugly words
back. The sense of inadequacy she'd felt when Eddie died and
the air force uncovered the true story was as devastating today
as it had been when she was a nineteen-year-old girl who
believed in fairy tales and happy endings.

Let her mother look for orange blossoms and double-ring
ceremonies, for happiness to come in the guise of a strong pair
of shoulders. Joanna knew better.

Or at least she thought she did.

Just how Ryder O'Neal had managed to get under her skin
like that, to probe so close to the secret part of her heart that
had died along with Eddie, was a mystery better left unsolved.

She'd worked too hard to regain her sense of self and she
wasn't about to let an ill-advised confession undermine the
long years of growth.

"He was a damned fool," Ryder said. His cane scraped
against the polished wood floor. "You know that, don't you?"

She turned around. "I know it now." She'd already said
more than enough. There was no way on earth she was about
to tell him about the darker times when she'd sought self-
esteem in the arms of other men, only to pull away at any hint
of real commitment. She'd acquired a reputation as a heart-
breaker but hers was the only heart that had actually ever
broken.

He glanced across the room at the eight-day clock that
rested on the mantel over the fireplace. "It's late. I'd better
get moving."

She forced a smile. "Busy day tomorrow?"

He smiled back. "You know how it is for us idle rich. Gotta
keep American Express in business."

"No, you don't," she said as she walked him to the door. "I manage to do that single-handedly."

The look he gave her reached deep into the shadows of her heart. "Why do I think that's the way you do most things?"

She said nothing. His accuracy stunned her.

"Am I wrong?"

There was no sense denying it. "How did you know?"

"I have good instincts."

"I'll keep that in mind." X-ray vision you could protect yourself against. X-ray instincts left you defenseless, and Joanna hated being defenseless more than anything on earth.

"There's something else."

She tensed. "Another observation?"

He adjusted his cane. "Of a different nature."

She tried to draw a deep breath but the look in his eyes made it impossible.

"We would have been good together."

"I beg your pardon?"

He smiled. "You were thinking that before, weren't you?"

Why try to deny it? The red flush covering her body was proof positive. "Yes. Are you psychic?" If he was, maybe the surgeon general should stamp a warning on his forehead to alert unsuspecting women given to flights of fantasy.

Those oddly beautiful hazel eyes of his seemed able to pierce right through her protective armor—whether she wanted them to or not.

"I'm not psychic," he said, never taking his gaze from her face. "I fantasize, too."

The powerful image of herself moving beneath him made her body feel touched by fire. She wasn't a naive schoolgirl, nor was she unaware of the pure power of desire for its own sake. But articulating her fantasies in the foyer of her mother's apartment was beyond her. Especially when the object of those fantasies was looking at her as if she were naked and he, ready for anything.

She gestured toward the crazily decorated cast on his right leg. "I edited out your broken leg."

"Good move," he said, his voice lower, deeper than before. "I gave us a big, wide bed and lots of time."

Her heart pounded wildly at all her pulse points in a way that was almost painful. "It was dark. Just the light from the moon and the stars."

"No, Joanna." Although he didn't move closer, she felt as if she'd been drawn into his embrace. "The light in the room is on. I want to be able to see you."

Desire, hot and wild, swept over her, and made her tremble with need.

Stop this, she thought. She was losing control, losing the cool air of reserve she'd worked so hard to acquire, the reserve that gave her the upper hand in relationships with men, the reserve that made it possible for her to make certain she would never be hurt again.

"Sorry to disappoint you," she said, "but I like it with the lights out."

"Is that negotiable?"

"Afraid not."

"I'm sorry," he said.

"So am I."

"We could have made each other very happy, Joanna."

She closed her eyes for a moment. "I know." Her entire body hungered for him.

And then, before she could think, he leaned forward and kissed her swiftly on the mouth.

He was gone before she realized just how much she'd wanted him to ask her one more time.

"You're a fool," Ryder muttered as he pushed the elevator button for the eleventh floor. "A goddamned idiot."

The erotic possibilities between them as they'd stood in the hallway of her mother's apartment had been limitless. Not even Alistair and one of his state-of-the-art computers could possibly have measured the throbbing, liquid tension that had polarized them, promising everything but ultimately delivering nothing at all.

He'd been around long enough to know that if he'd pursued her, pulled Joanna into his arms on that overstuffed sofa and let his hands and mouth explore her body, those fantasies they'd spoken about would have become reality.

Where Valerie had been open and vulnerable years ago, so he was now. At first he'd thought he backed away from Joanna to save her from certain pain; now he recognized that for the sham it was.

When she told him the room would be dark with only moonlight to guide them, he'd hardened in anticipation, and it had taken a supreme act of will to keep from sliding his hands up under that loose-fitting silk shirt of hers.

But even after he'd given her pleasure and had been pleasured by her, as well, it wouldn't have been enough. He would want her again and again, an endless chain of days and nights of wanting her body, her heart and her soul.

He'd known women as beautiful before; he'd known women just as witty and twice as willing. But he'd never come so far so fast, never been allowed to see beyond the facade and view the beating, fragile wonder of the human heart as he had tonight with Joanna. That simple act of exposing her soul had done more to seal his fate than any act of sex.

The elevator doors opened and he headed down the hallway toward his PAX-provided apartment, pulling his PAX-provided key out of his pocket and inserting it into the PAX-provided lock.

He'd lived in a rarefied atmosphere for so long his lungs didn't know what to do with air down at sea level. What in hell did he know about reality? For the past fifteen years he'd been guided and molded and encouraged by the best and the brightest the Western nations had to offer. His talents had guided the destinies of a score of countries. The lives of the great and the near-great had rested in his hands.

But when it came down to it, love was the deadliest emotion of them all, because it was the only one that held the power to destroy.

Chapter Eight

Another old wives' tale bit the dust.

Cold showers didn't work.

One hour after Ryder left, Joanna toweled herself off and slipped into one of Cynthia's countless silky bathrobes that occupied a full third of the walk-in closet in the master bedroom. Cynthia might be a lunatic when it came to affairs of the heart, but there was something to be said for being the daughter of a devout Sybarite. The slither of satin against Joanna's skin was delicious—almost as delicious as the feel of Ryder's mouth on hers.

"Dangerous thoughts," she said out loud as she headed toward the kitchen and her long-forgotten dinner. Too dangerous to let get out of hand.

She'd be damned if she allowed herself to become involved with a man who was as obviously wrong for her as Ryder O'Neal. One mistake in a lifetime was more than enough.

It wasn't hard to see that Ryder was everything she'd been avoiding all these years, the reason she'd avoided actors and other charismatic types she worked with and gravitated toward attorneys and businessmen, men who were sedate and safe in their three-piece suits. Men she could outrun and outmaneuver and forget as quickly as she herself was forgotten. There was a certain security in knowing that by lowering your hopes, you also lowered your chances of being hurt.

Ryder O'Neal was witty and independent and unlikely to

be bothered with petty things like commitment and security. Unfortunately, Joanna had learned just how important those petty things were to her.

She'd learned it the hard way.

It HAD BEEN the rainiest November in New York history and Thanksgiving Day was no exception.

All through dinner, Joanna Stratton Carr had tried to pretend that it was a normal family celebration but the gloomy weather more than matched her mood.

Her mother had flitted in and out of the enormous kitchen, supervising the caterer and his assistants, while Mark Van-Dyke, her third husband, argued with Eddie about Vietnam. Eddie, dressed in his Army uniform, did his best to stick up for the government's point of view, but Joanna could tell by the twitch in his left shoulder that Mark's stinging comments got under Eddie's skin.

A hell of a way for a young married couple to spend their last few hours together. The minutes were slipping away faster than Joanna could pull them back in a desperate attempt to hang on to this first bit of security she'd ever known. Despite these frequent U.S. Army-induced separations, Eddie Carr represented a safe haven, true love, the prospect of a home and family—all the things she'd dreamed of as a little girl.

When the taxi came to take Eddie to the airport, Joanna was practically in tears.

"Don't go," she said, as they embraced in the lobby of the Carillon. "Stay just one more night, Eddie. You don't have to report to San Francisco until Saturday morning." She kissed his cheek, his jaw, his throat. "We'll stay in a hotel. We'll—" She whispered something in his ear so the doorman wouldn't hear her.

Eddie, however, had obviously already made his break from civilian life. He removed her hands from around his neck and kissed each palm.

"You're making it harder on me, Jo." His voice sounded far away.

"Good. I want to make it hard so you won't leave me."
Don't leave me, Eddie. I can't live without you.

"I don't have any choice. You know that."

"A few more hours then, Eddie. Just a few more hours."
They'd been married less than a year and, thanks to Uncle
Sam, had been apart more than half of that time. PFC Edward
Carr was the first wonderful thing to ever happen to Joanna
Stratton, and she was young enough and naive enough to be-
lieve that she could succeed where her mother had failed re-
peatedly. "I need you more than the Army does." *Don't make
me step back into Cynthia's life when I want my own.*

He'd simply looked at her, his dark brown eyes unreadable,
then smiled that long, lazy smile that had twisted her stomach
into knots the first night they met. Joanna and her mother were
alike in that one respect: Both women were suckers for a pretty
face.

"Just six months, Jo," he said, pushing her long black hair
away from her eyes, "and I'll have R and R in Hawaii. You
can meet me there."

It didn't matter that between them they had barely enough
money for the cab ride to JFK, much less Joanna's plane fare
to Hawaii. His words were exactly what she needed to hear—
and what she wanted to believe.

"I'll drop out of school and get a job," she said. "If I live
with Cynthia and Mark while you're away, we can save a
fortune." That wonderful Cape Cod house in Levittown with
the white picket fence might someday become a reality.

He smiled but she could tell his mind was far away.

Next to them, the doorman discreetly cleared his throat.
"Your taxi's here, folks."

Eddie pulled Joanna to him, and she closed her eyes and
began to cry. For eighteen years she'd searched for someone
to love her the way Eddie loved her, someone who would
protect her and cherish her, all the things she'd longed for as
a child but never found.

"Everything will be fine," Eddie said, kissing her for the
very last time. "I'll be back before you know it."

And he was.

He died two days later in a car crash just outside San Antonio, Texas, while driving his pregnant girlfriend to her obstetrician's office.

Private First Class Edward Joseph Carr came back home on Sunday, November 25. He was buried on Tuesday, November 27 in Pine Lawn Cemetery.

The last of Joanna's illusions were buried along with him.

"DAMN IT!" Joanna slammed her fist down on the kitchen counter and curled up on the window seat overlooking the street in front of the Carillon.

Why couldn't Ryder O'Neal be an investment banker or an English professor or a periodontist? Why couldn't he be tweedy and weathered and content to sit before a fire with Joanna on his left and an Irish setter on his right? She wanted a man to share her life with, not one who would keep his own counsel.

Mysterious, handsome strangers were wonderful heroes in the movies, but they made lousy partners in real life. That was why she'd made it a point to spurn the advances of the show business types she came in contact with on the job and to limit her romances to the men who came more conservatively packaged.

She'd needed to reestablish herself both as a woman and as a person and it had taken many years—and a few mistakes—to understand exactly what she needed. Casual romances had their place, but they no longer had a place in her life.

Her mother or Holland would be able to view an interlude with someone like Ryder O'Neal as just that—a blissful vacation from real life. For Joanna that would be impossible because, no matter how logically her mind worked, her terribly illogical heart would do her in every time.

WHAT RYDER NEEDED was a large glass of Scotch; what he didn't need was Alistair Chambers.

However, like it or not, there the Englishman sat, ensconced in the leather wing chair near the window with his ubiquitous brandy in hand, listening to Beethoven and waiting for Ryder to come home.

"Goddamn it, Chambers!" Ryder flung his crutches to the floor and hobbled over to the bar to pour himself some Chivas Regal. "You have ten phones in that Rolls of yours. Don't any of them work?"

"They're only truly effective when the other party deigns to pick up the receiver. Nasty complication, that." He switched off the stereo system. "You've been playing hard to get tonight, my boy."

"It's known as privacy." Ryder sat down on the sofa and put his right leg up on the glass table in front of him. "I'm acquiring a taste for it."

Ryder quickly downed his drink. He usually didn't allow himself such bravura displays of macho behavior but, damn it, it was one of those nights.

"You don't gulp Chivas; you savor it," Alistair said. "You colonials lack common sense when it comes to the finer things."

"Stuff it, Chambers. We had sense enough to rebel from British domination, didn't we?"

"Is that what this show of independence is all about then— a throwback to revolutionary glory."

"If you've finished analyzing my behavior, why don't you tell me what the hell you're doing in my apartment."

"I would think my purpose is painfully obvious."

"I've had a tough night, Chambers. I'm not in the mood for guessing games."

Alistair stood up, and fished in his breast pocket for one of those foul-smelling foreign cigarettes Ryder despised. "Things have heated up on St. George. I have the plane waiting at the airport."

"How serious is it?"

Alistair took a long drag on his cigarette, then let the pale blue smoke out slowly. "Code 5." Critical but not dire.

"I'll go."

Alistair, who rarely showed any emotion much less down-right surprise, stared at Ryder. "What?"

"Just give me five minutes to grab a shower and we'll leave."

The older man shook his head. "You haven't even allowed me the pleasure of launching into my 'you-owe-it-to-the-organization' speech."

Ryder pulled himself up from the couch. "You can give it to me in the limo on the way to JFK."

"I must say you've taken some of the joy out of this tri-umph, Ryder. Is this a permanent change of heart or just your basic humanitarian instincts rearing their head?"

Twenty-four hours ago Ryder would have tossed the urbane Mr. Chambers out on his elegant ass by way of an answer. But that was before he met Joanna Stratton, before he'd seen his future stretching out before him all shiny and new and his for the taking.

Before he'd realized how big a coward he really was.

The situation in St. George was serious; there was no de-nying that the lives of a score of innocent people hung in the balance. Why then did Ryder feel more like he was running away from something than running to help?

"Ryder?" Alistair's voice was quizzical, concerned.

"I don't know," Ryder said finally as he headed for the shower. *I don't know one damned thing anymore.*

"I THOUGHT you had an audition this morning," Joanna said when Holland showed up on her doorstep at the ungodly hour of nine. She covered her mouth and yawned as Holland, gor-geous even in her running outfit, swept into the apartment. "I wish you'd phoned."

"I'm too distraught to make phone calls," Holland said.

"What's the problem?" She followed Holland into the kitchen, abandoning all hope of going back to sleep. "Don't tell me you lost the job already."

Holland pulled a bottle of Bloody Mary mix out of the refrigerator and plucked a clean glass from the dishwasher while Joanna slumped onto a kitchen chair.

"The audition's this afternoon," Holland said distractedly. "That's not my problem."

Joanna watched her friend pour the thick red juice into a glass and winced. "Don't ask me where the vodka is. My stomach couldn't take it this early."

"Then look the other way." Holland pulled a tiny airline-size bottle of Stolichnaya from her gym bag and added it to the Bloody Mary mix. "This is an emergency."

Joanna groaned and got up to start some coffee. "What on earth is the matter with you? Did you lose your union card or just your marbles?"

Holland took a long sip of her drink. "I shall endeavor to ignore your sarcasm, my dear Joanna."

Joanna leaned against the sink and stared at her friend. "'I shall endeavor to ignore…'?" Despite the early hour, she threw back her head and laughed. "One night with the debonair Mr. Chambers and you're ready for *Masterpiece Theater.*"

"Correction: One *evening* with Mr. Chambers. His night remained his own." Holland sighed. "Not, I might add, from lack of trying."

"Oh, no." Joanna plugged in the Mr. Coffee machine and sat back down at the table. "Don't tell me he's gay."

Holland made a face, then quickly smoothed the faint lines on her forehead with her index fingers. "I almost hope he is. That, at least, I can understand."

"What exactly happened?"

"We went to Le Cirque. We drank. We ate. We danced until midnight, then, poof! He disappeared like Cinderella after the ball." Holland's laugh was shaky. "I almost expected my cab to turn into a pumpkin."

"Maybe he doesn't kiss on the first date," Joanna said, trying to make light of Holland's obvious distress. "Maybe he's playing hard to get."

Holland drooped over her Bloody Mary like a wilted stalk of celery. "And maybe he's already 'gotten.'"

"No," Joanna said. "He's not married."

Holland perked up. "How do you know?"

Ryder O'Neal was the one topic Joanna wanted to steer clear of, but it was too late. "I asked his friend."

Holland patted her right leg. "You mean that gorgeous specimen with the broken leg you were with yesterday?"

Joanna nodded. "That's the one."

"You realize if I wasn't in such an extreme state of emotional turmoil I would ask you why you were walking the streets made up like a bag lady, don't you?"

"I was trying out my makeup techniques," Joanna said, glad to steer the conversation away from talk of Ryder. "I did a damned good job, too, if I do say so myself."

"Unless you have that gorgeous specimen hidden in the bedroom, I'd say you did too good a job." Holland got up and poured them each a cup of coffee. "How did you manage to keep from yanking off that god-awful wig and throwing yourself into his muscular arms?"

"Superior self-control," Joanna said dryly. "Not to mention the fact that I'd have probably put him into cardiac arrest with that move."

"Maybe," Holland said, sitting back down, "but think of what fun you could have had administering CPR."

Joanna tore open a blue packet of Equal and dumped it into her coffee. "You know what your problem is, don't you? You're man crazy."

Holland flashed Joanna one of her best smiles. "I don't deny it," she said. "And until I find a man who's crazy about only me, I intend to stay this way." She reached for one of the bagels Joanna had put out on the table. "It's one of the last bastions of defense left to womankind."

Joanna grabbed a bagel for herself and laughed, glad that the subject of Ryder O'Neal had been successfully bypassed. "You realize I don't have any idea what in hell you're talking about, don't you?"

Of course, when Holland Masters was on a roll, it hardly mattered. She launched into an elaborate and highly theatrical discourse on sexual politics that had Joanna holding her sides against the laughter. Holland didn't stop for breath until there was a knock on Joanna's door.

"Hold that thought," Joanna said. "It's probably just Stanley about the leaky bathroom faucet."

"I hope he didn't bring those two new sleazeballs he hired with him," Holland said as Joanna tightened the belt on her robe and went to the door. "There's something awfully sinister about them."

The two young men Joanna had seen in the mail room with Stanley might have been unpleasant but sinister was hardly a word she would apply to them.

"You're just a snob," Joanna called out over her shoulder as she opened the door. "If a man isn't in Harris tweeds, he's an escaped felon."

"An escaped felon?" Rosie Callahan, still tall and imposing in her aged mink coat, stood on the doorstep, carrying a pecan coffee ring fresh from the bakery down the block. "That sounds interesting. Anyone I know?"

"I wouldn't be surprised," Joanna said, motioning her inside. "You seem to know everyone in town."

Rosie's laugh was loud and hearty.

"I'd know that sound anywhere," Holland called out. "Come on in, Rosie, and join the party."

"A party, is it?" Rosie said, heading toward the kitchen. "You should have told me, Joanna. I would have dressed for the occasion."

"This wasn't my idea," Joanna said, taking down some plates from the cupboard over the sink. "This seems to be my day for attracting uninvited guests."

"Excuse me," Holland said, plucking a big pecan from the coffee cake and popping it into her mouth. "Uninvited guests have feelings, too, Stratton."

Rosie shot Joanna a knowing look. "It's not the uninvited

guests who interest me. I want to know about the guest you
did invite in last night.''

Joanna kept her expression blank. ''Whatever do you mean,
Rosie?''

''Yes, Rosie,'' Holland said, her eyes twinkling. ''Whatever
do you mean?''

If she hadn't been so sleepy, Joanna could have cheerfully
taken both her friends and tossed them out her ninth-floor window without a second thought.

''Well, after Joanna left last night,'' Rosie said, slicing herself a generous piece of the pecan ring, ''I went out to the
incinerator to check for my girdles—''

Holland turned to Joanna. ''Check for her girdles?''

''It's a long story,'' Joanna said. ''Trust me.''

Rosie cleared her throat. ''As I was saying, I went to the
incinerator to check for my girdles when I heard the elevator
open. Now those two new helpers Stanley hired have been
doing an awful lot of prowling around this building lately—
and I never liked men with red hair—so I picked up the broom
that Mr. Mott in 917 was throwing out and was ready to go
at it when I saw Ryder heading for Joanna's door, carrying a
bottle of wine and looking as happy as you please.''

Holland leaned forward. ''Ryder-with-the-broken-leg Ryder?''

''Who else?'' Joanna muttered. ''My life is an open book.''

''Anyway,'' Rosie went on, ''he saw me standing just inside
the door of the incinerator room and he gave me the biggest
smile I've seen since Mary Tyler Moore went off the air.''

''That's a terrible analogy, Rosie,'' said Joanna. ''Couldn't
you have picked a male star, at least?''

''I think the analogy is wonderful,'' Holland said. ''Who
has more teeth than Mary Tyler Moore?''

''Now, I don't know what happened while he was in here,
Jo—''

Joanna muttered ''Thank God'' under her breath.

''—but I do know what happened afterward. At precisely
3:23 a.m. on the GE alarm clock that I bought on sale at

Alexander's last week, Ryder O'Neal and that dapper English fellow, Alistair Something-or-other, climbed into that snazzy Rolls-Royce I've seen before and drove off.'' Rosie, whose blood still ran thick with greasepaint, paused for dramatic effect. ''And,'' she said slowly, ''he hasn't come back home yet.''

Before Joanna could begin to make sense out of Rosie's stream-of-consciousness news bulletin, Holland let out a moan and buried her face in her hands.

''Oh, my God,'' Holland said, her voice strangled. ''They're in love!''

Chapter Nine

At that exact moment, Ryder was cursing Alistair Chambers, PAX and his own shortcomings for getting him into this situation.

He was 150 yards away from the American embassy where a radical group—insanely determined to drive the U.S. and her tourist dollars out of St. George—was threatening to blow up the embassy building and the surrounding villas.

Although it was just seven in the morning, the blistering Caribbean sun beat down on his back as he crawled through the underbrush, slapping away assorted tropical pests, as he made his way toward the spot where he would set up his equipment. He'd demanded to be cut out of his cast two days early and now his leg, stiff and tender from weeks of disuse, dragged behind him, slowing him down.

Joanna Stratton and the night before seemed light-years away.

This was reality, the one thing he was good at, the one thing he knew he could handle.

Strapped to his back was a million dollars' worth of technical hardware designed to defuse an explosive from up to two hundred yards away. It was the backbone of PAX's extensive antiterriorist paraphernalia—and Ryder's proudest achievement to date. Using the latest information on the terrorists who were holed up in the embassy, he had fed all his information into the computer terminal on the flight down to St. George and had come up with a series of variables delineating the probable type, amount and composition of the explosive he was up against.

The beauty of his system was its flexibility; the program actually took into account the human element of unpredictablity. It had worked flawlessly at the Cannes Film Festival when an Arab extremist group threatened the U.S. filmmakers, as well as during an unpublicized attack against the U.S. Senate that had come closer to full-fledged disaster than Ryder cared think about.

Alistair's voice crackled through the tiny receiver attached to the inner curve of Ryder's right ear. "Ten more meters to the right will bring you in line. Set it up, then move fifteen degrees due east. Foster will be there to pick you up."

Ryder, who was outfitted with a sophisticated communications system the size of a peppercorn, had only to tap his thumbnail to this watchband twice to signal receipt of Alistair's message.

He was almost there.

According to the terrorists' threats, the bombs were set to explode in eighteen minutes. According to Ryder's calculations, he would have the system programmed in and fully operational within thirteen minutes; the bomb would be defused two minutes later.

Not much of a margin for error, but then, Ryder O'Neal had never needed one.

Seventeen minutes and counting...

PAX NEVER STAYED around long enough to take a bow.

Ryder and Alistair were back in their private jet and lifting up into the skies above St. George before handcuffs were slapped on the last of the terrorists.

Ryder was flying high himself on a mixture of relief and excitement.

"The possibilities are limitless," he said, pacing up and down the plushly carpeted cabin. "This was the toughest time limit we've ever worked under and with the least information—if it worked this time, it'll work every time."

Alistair watched him carefully, his blue eyes guarded and thoughtful. "I know what you're thinking," he said, "and it can't be done."

"The hell it can't. Nothing's impossible."

"Detecting the existence of plastic explosives is impossible, Ryder. Israel came close three years ago but the variables were too many to make it feasible. England managed one improvement on the Israeli formula but the limitations outweighed the advantages."

"I think I can do it." It had taken returning to his old life to discover the key to a new one.

Alistair's expression didn't change. "Is this your adrenaline speaking or the Scotch?"

"Neither," Ryder said. "It was being out there today." He explained the idea that had crystallized for him as he set up the equipment outside the embassy in clear, simple terms. "Given the molecular structure, it should work."

"That's an enormous project you're talking about, Ryder. Things change so quickly, the other side would be onto something new before you even got set up."

He wasn't about to tell his friend that his idea was almost operational. His recuperation period hadn't been wasted. "Worth the risk, wouldn't you say?"

Plastic explosives were the most insidious of all terrorist tactics. Opening a letter, taking the cap off a can of deodorant, twisting a tube of lipstick—in the hands of a madman, each simple action could mean death to scores of innocent people. The benefits of a device like the one Ryder outlined would be incalculable.

Ryder could see Alistair's mind weighing the issues involved and he waited for the result.

"I can't deny that what you've outlined shows promise, Ryder, but I feel there is more here than meets the eye." Alistair leaned back and lit a cigarette, an obvious bid for time.

Ryder knew he had his old friend exactly where he wanted him. "Do you want me to jump right to the bottom line?"

A cloud of smoke wreathed Alistair's head as he spoke. "Yes."

"If I come up with a viable device, I get to write my own ticket from there on."

Alistair threw his head back and laughed. "Come now, my boy. You already write your own ticket. You have for years. Look at that apartment at the Carillon, your place in Hawaii, your—"

"I'm not talking about possessions," Ryder broke in. "I'm talking about my freedom."

Alistair sighed. "You sound like a dissident seeking safe haven. I wish you would find other words."

"Okay," he said. "I'm talking about the rest of my life. I want to work on my projects and then train other people to implement them." He drew in a deep breath. "I want to stay in one place for the first time in my adult life and find out what in hell the real world is like. Damn it, Chambers! I want what you had—someone to love."

"Nothing lasts," Alistair said. "There's little enough out there to compare to what the organization can offer, Ryder."

Ryder thought about Joanna Stratton; in just a few hours she'd made him feel more alive, more eager than he had in years. He wanted the chance to explore that better part of himself that she seemed to reach so effortlessly.

"I'm willing to risk it." He put his hand on the older man's shoulder. "You had your chance," he said, referring to Alistair's late wife, Sarah. "Now I'd like to have mine."

ALISTAIR CHAMBERS LOVED Ryder as he would have loved the son he'd never had. It was the one weak spot in an otherwise perfectly seamless image. Nurturing Ryder's genius, introducing him to the world, seeing him develop into one of the most important components—albeit incognito—on the scene filled him with tremendous pleasure.

Ryder was the one bright spot in a life that had been emotionally arid since his Sarah died nine years ago. All of the deeper feelings his vocation frowned upon normally had found their expression in his mentor/protégé relationship with this brilliant young man.

The thought of losing him to a laboratory pained him but he fought it down. It would be years before even a genius like O'Neal could bring that dream to life. Maybe by then Alistair would be retired to his London home, living the life of a cultured gentleman of leisure with a beautiful, witty woman like Holland Masters by his side who—

But that was neither here nor there. The laboratory was a metaphor for something much larger, something much more important. Ryder was beginning to chafe against the anonymous nature of his life. Continuity and permanence—things he had so blithely disregarded years ago—suddenly beckoned.

It came with age. It came with ennui. It came, sometimes, in the form of a woman. He remembered Valerie Parker and Ryder's cavalier attitude toward love.

The Ryder O'Neal who thought he needed nothing but his genius was not the same Ryder O'Neal who stood before him today. Sooner or later, it all came down to the basics.

Men and women needed each other. They always had. They always would.

And there was nothing in Alistair's considerable bag of tricks that could begin to change that simple fact.

"Agreed," he said, finishing his drink and putting the glass back down on the table next to his chair. "If you can pull this off, we'll think about setting you up with the internal organization as a consultant."

"I'll pull it off," Ryder said. "Mark my words. You won't regret this decision."

Strange, Alistair thought. He'd regretted so many of the others. Why should this one be any different?

NOW JOANNA DIDN'T for a moment believe that Ryder O'Neal and the elegant Alistair Chambers were in anything remotely resembling love, but it tickled her to let Holland Masters ruminate on that possibility.

After the impromptu breakfast club meeting, Rosie had left to prepare for her Friday departure to visit Bert Higgins in Florida. Holland was going back downtown to prepare for her audition, and Joanna, who needed supplies from Ranaghan's House of Makeup and Magic, shared a cab with her.

"I should have known better," Holland said, as the cab lurched through traffic around Penn Station. "When will I ever learn? The best ones are always taken." She looked over at Joanna and rolled her eyes. "One way or another."

While Holland rambled on about the inequities of life, Joanna tried to piece together the clues. She'd worked with enough actors whose macho public personas shielded very private desires, to know the real thing when she met him. Ryder O'Neal was a normal, functioning, heterosexual male; of that, she had no doubt.

What confused her was his relationship to the urbane and elegant Alistair Chambers, whose Rolls-Royce, according to Rosie Callahan, was a daily fixture in front of the Carillon.

"Maybe he's his financial advisor," Joanna said as they inched their way through the lower East Side.

Holland stopped in midsentence. "What?"

"Maybe Alistair is Ryder's financial advisor."

"A financial advisor who drives a Rolls?"

Joanna shrugged. "A very successful advisor."

"No," Holland said, "the Rolls has to belong to your friend with the cast. I see Alistair as the family attorney."

"He's not the legal type," Joanna said. "Did you see that red handkerchief in his breast pocket? Too whimsical."

Holland's shoulders drooped. "That leaves only one more alternative, Joanna. They're—"

"Business partners!" Joanna sat straight up in her seat. "They're working on an important deal that requires daily consultation. And since Ryder doesn't have an office, they meet at his apartment."

Holland brightened. "Ryder's broken leg makes it impossible for him to get to Alistair's office." They both blithely overlooked the fact that Ryder and his crutches managed to navigate the city quite nicely. "The deal is hot and Alistair, wonderful man that he is, makes the supreme sacrifice and goes to Ryder."

"And Ryder, ever the humanitarian, sends the Rolls for him."

"There's still one problem."

"I know." Joanna braced herself as the cab screeched to a halt at a red light. "What business could they possibly have accomplished at three in the morning?"

"Everything I can think of is illegal."

"I'm sure there's a logical explanation," Joanna said, pushing thoughts of megadollar drug deals and international scam operations from her mind. "Maybe they were heading for one of those after-hours clubs near SoHo."

"I'd rather find out they were smuggling counterfeit Calvin Klein jeans to the disadvantaged in the Soviet Union." Holland groaned as the cab made a sharp left and she was thrown against the door handle. "What did your pal O'Neal say he did for a living?"

"He said he was rich. What did Chambers say he did?"

"He said he was an associate of O'Neal's."

"Wait a minute," Joanna said, as a thought came to her. "When I was in my Kathryn costume, he mentioned that he and Chambers were in business together."

Holland leaned forward eagerly. "In business doing what?"

As if on cue, a New York City fire truck roared past them and Joanna gestured in its direction. "Fighting fires."

"They work for the fire department?" Holland waved her hands in disgust. "Really, Joanna, I—"

"I'm giving you an exact quote. He said, 'fighting fires.'"

"What the hell does that mean?" Holland's sophisticated demeanor fell apart before her frustration.

"I have no idea."

"You didn't ask?"

"I didn't have time. The next second I saw you standing

there with Alistair and I was too preoccupied with keeping you from blowing my cover.''

"Blowing your cover?'' Holland laughed. "When did you join the CIA?''

"Just a figure of speech.''

"So, why didn't you follow up on it later?''

"I was too busy defending my honor.''

Holland looked horrified. "He made a *pass* at you while you were in old-age makeup?''

Joanna sighed. The thought of explaining the whole foolish story about the blind date mix-up and her own wounded ego was exhausting. "It's a long story,'' she said as the cab screeched to a stop in front of Ranaghan's. She pulled a ten-dollar bill out of her pocket and handed it to Holland for her part of the fare. "Believe me, it's not as awful as it sounds.''

"Everything's as awful as it sounds,'' Holland said. "Why couldn't they be stockbrokers? At least you know where stockbrokers are at three in the morning.''

"My sentiments exactly,'' Joanna said as she got out of the cab. "I'll call you later.''

THE TAXI ROCKETED OFF into traffic and Holland leaned back against the seat and massaged her aching temples.

She felt as if she'd been through three open auditions, five callbacks and a phone call with her invisible agent, and it wasn't even noon yet.

Joanna in old-age makeup. Decadently expensive Rolls-Royces. Missing girdles. Gorgeous men who not only didn't kiss and tell—they didn't kiss at all. Fighting fires at three a.m.

It was too much.

She'd rather be trapped in an Ibsen play than go through another twenty-four hours like this. Her evening with Alistair Chambers had been something out of a Judith Krantz novel: exciting, glamorous and tinged with enough mystery that she could barely speak on the way back to her apartment.

When he left her chastely at the doorstep she'd wanted to

throw a shoe at his departing head. Men like Alistair Chambers were few and far between; she'd been around long enough to know that for a fact. Short of doing the Dance of the Seven Veils in the hallway, she couldn't have made her intentions more obvious.

However, as the saying went, you could lead a man to water, but—

"To hell with you, Alistair Chambers," she said, ignoring the cabby's curious glance in the rearview mirror. "To bloody hell with you."

If he got his jollies fighting fires with men who wore psychedelic casts, that was his problem. Holland would do just fine without him.

The cab slammed its way through a pothole the size of an open manhole cover and she lurched forward, hitting her knees against the back of the seat in front of her.

Rubbing her left knee, she laughed out loud. Some people liked leather. Some people liked lace. Maybe Alistair Chambers had a thing for plaster of paris.

This was New York. Anything was possible.

And in New York, the competition was fierce. If there was one thing she'd learned during her checkered acting career, it was the importance of dressing the part.

Men like Alistair Chambers came along once in a lifetime, if you were lucky.

Holland thought of Joanna and her Kathryn Hayes getup and wondered how she herself would look with a nice little *removable* cast on her right wrist.

Then she wondered if maybe it was time to start thinking about a nice, long vacation.

RANAGHAN'S HOUSE of Makeup and Magic had everything Joanna needed and more. By the time she staggered out to the street to hail a cab home to the Carillon, her bags were heavy and her pocketbook light.

Her mood, however, hovered somewhere in between.

All the way back uptown, she replayed the scene in her

apartment the night before, trying to make sense out of what exactly had happened between her and Ryder O'Neal.

It was like trying to make sense out of a soap bubble.

The attraction between them had been as sudden and intense as a lightning storm. The words they spoke to each other were words of fantasy and desire. Nothing in her experience had prepared her for the suddenness and force of her unbridled emotions.

Only the imaginary grandmother in the back room had kept Joanna from moving into his arms as naturally as day moves into night.

His leaving town with Alistair Chambers was the best thing that could have happened to her.

Now, the trick was in convincing herself to believe it.

She paid the cabdriver, then lugged her packages through the lobby of the Carillon. The red-haired workmen were doing something with the lighting in the mail room and, not anxious to be scrutinized like meat in the butcher case, Joanna put off getting her mail until later.

She was juggling her packages and trying to press the elevator button when someone stepped up behind her and took one of the bags from her hand.

"You look like you're havin' trouble, Ms. Stratton." Stanley stood smiling at her side. "Let me help."

"No need," she said, despite the fact her need was obvious. "I can manage."

He didn't relinquish her bags. "It isn't often I get to help a lovely lady such as yourself," he said, in a clumsy attempt at gallantry that was marred by the look in his eyes. "Let me."

She was aware of his two workmen listening avidly a few feet away. A patent dismissal of Stanley's help might be unwise. The elevator door slid open.

"Thank you."

They stepped inside and Stanley pushed the button marked nine.

"How is Mrs. del Portago enjoyin' her trip?" he asked as another tenant got in at the second floor.

She thought about yesterday's letter, which detailed Stavros's biceps in excruciating detail. "She's having the time of her life."

"Nice woman, your mother," Stanley continued, watching Joanna who was watching him. "Never any hassles with her. Always got time to talk."

Joanna nodded. Cynthia had her problems but getting along with men wasn't among them. Her particular brand of charm was especially effective with working-class types like Stanley Holt.

The other tenant got off at the fifth floor.

Stanley waited for the doors to close before he continued. "Now, that Rosie Callahan is something else."

Instantly Joanna went on alert. "Rosie is quite an extraordinary woman."

"Oh, yeah, Mrs. Callahan's a live one. Don't get me wrong, I like her a whole lot. But, livin' alone like she does—well, she's not gettin' any younger, Ms. Stratton. I think she's—" He hesitated.

"You think she's what?"

"Forgetful. I mean, in the past few weeks I spent more time chasin' down her lost stuff than doin' what I have to do around the building. The boss don't like it when those stairs aren't spit-shined." Stanley grinned and she shuddered inside.

The elevator stopped at the ninth floor and Joanna exited first.

"What exactly are you saying, Stanley?" she asked as she fished in her pocket for her house keys.

He put down her packages in front of her door and faced her. "I'm sayin' she should be careful." His voice was even and he was smiling, but his words carried a subliminal threat. "Those fliers of hers could get a lady into big trouble. Life is tough for people like Rosie. I don't want to see it get any tougher." She opened the door and he moved aside. "You know what I mean, Ms. Stratton?"

"No," she said, meeting his eyes. "I can't say that I do."

"Rosie will. You just pass on the message." He touched

the bill of his baseball cap with two fingers. "Have a nice day."

With that, he disappeared down the fire stairs.

"Pompous jackass," Joanna mumbled as she dragged her packages into her apartment.

"Idiotic, arrogant fool," she was still mumbling when she sat down in front of her lighted mirror to perfect her old-age makeup for the assignment next week.

How wonderful it would be to walk up to Stanley—in her full Kathryn Hayes regalia—and punch him right in the mouth.

Now that was something she *would* remember to tell Rosie.

Chapter Ten

"How do people on Long Island stand this?" Ryder asked as the Rolls-Royce snaked it way through the clot of traffic on the expressway. "If I had to commute through this twice a day, I'd go nuts."

Alistair lit one of his foreign cigarettes and glanced at two truck drivers arguing over a fender bender at the side of the road. "Real life," he said, smoke encircling his head. "This is what you've been pining for, my boy."

Ryder, displaying unusual restraint, let the remark pass. Their jet had whisked them back from St. George in less time than it was taking them to make their way from MacArthur Airport to Manhattan. The wonders of the age of technology...

"You're certain I can't convince you to join me for a late lunch at the club?" Alistair asked. "After your exploits this morning, you've earned it."

"Not today." Ryder gestured toward his newly mobile right leg. "I'm out of shape. I think I'll spend the afternoon walking."

Alistair seemed thoughtful. "Anywhere in particular?"

Ryder arched an eyebrow in his direction. "I plan on doing ten laps around Columbus Avenue." He watched his colleague take a long, deliberate drag on his cigarette. "Am I under surveillance?"

Alistair chuckled but a pensive look remained in his blue eyes. "Nothing so sinister."

"Then why the interest in how I'll be spending my afternoon?"

"Would you believe me if I said normal curiosity?"

"I've known you too long," Ryder said. "Try something else."

Alistair stubbed out his cigarette in the built-in ashtray next to him. "Then I shall get right to the point: How well do you know Mrs. Kathryn Hayes?"

The question was so far out of left field that for a second Ryder didn't say anything. "Kathryn?"

Alistair nodded. "Your friend with the shopping cart."

"I don't know much of anything about her," he said, thinking back to their conversations. "She's seventy-seven years old and she's staying in her daughter's apartment."

"That's everything?"

"She likes having her way with elderly gentlemen." Alistair didn't laugh. Damn it, Ryder thought. He was getting too close. The last thing he wanted to do was talk about Joanna with Alistair.

There was no way Ryder could feign casual interest in front of the man who knew him so well.

"Does she have any other relatives?"

Bull's-eye. As soon as he got back to his apartment, Ryder was going to rip everything apart until he found the bugging equipment. In fact, knowing PAX, the whole damned building was probably bugged.

"You tell me," he said.

"No," Alistair countered. "I posed the question. Now you provide the answer."

"She has a granddaughter." He hesitated, not wanting to reveal the strange new emotions she'd brought out in him. "Her name is Joanna Stratton."

"Do you know what she does for a living?"

"She's a makeup artist." He regretted saying even that much when Alistair pulled out a slim leather notebook and made an entry. "What the hell's going on here anyway? Why the third degree?"

If Chambers told him Kathryn Hayes was an insurgent and Joanna, her accomplice—well, he wouldn't be held accountable for his actions.

Alistair put the notebook back in the breast pocket of his navy jacket. "I ran a check on Kathryn Hayes last night and a few items failed to add up. I'd like to run a new one."

"You ran a check?" Ryder slammed his hand against the plush door of the Rolls. "What the hell were you doing running a check? Were you afraid she had a pipe bomb in her shopping cart or a detonator in her support hose?"

"Are you forgetting the baby carriage with the plastic explosive in the Beirut airport?" Alistair's voice was quiet and matter-of-fact. "You're a valuable commodity to the other side, Ryder. Especially dead."

This was the first time in years that Ryder had actually spent any length of time with "civilians"; it was only natural for Alistair to be cautious. This, however, went beyond caution, and unfortunately, he knew that Alistair wouldn't have reacted that way without reason.

"I thought I was the best-kept secret in the organization," he said lightly. "No one outside of the top brass even knows my name." He leaned toward his mentor. "Has something gone down that I should know about?"

Alistair lit another cigarette. "Have you taken a good look at Mrs. Hayes's hands?"

"No," Ryder said, leaning back. "Have you checked your feet lately?"

"Amusing," said Alistair. "Now answer the question."

"I'll ask one of my own: Why the hell should I inspect Kathryn's hands?"

"Because seventy-eight—"

"Seventy-seven."

Alistair glared at him and went on. "Because seventy-seven-year-old women rarely have hands as smooth and un-marred as a girl's."

Ryder shrugged. "Maybe she uses Porcelana on them, or has good genes." He thought about her remarkably spry walk and uncommonly well-proportioned body, a body that Joanna seemed to have inherited. "Some traits seem to run in families."

"There's more to it than her hands, Ryder."

Ryder glanced out at the New York City skyline as they came off the Triborough Bridge and got onto the FDR Drive. "You're the one who ran a check on Kathryn. What did you find out?"

"You're not going to like it, my boy."

"I haven't liked any of this conversation so far. It hasn't stopped you yet."

"Kathryn Hayes died in 1981."

Ryder laughed. "I think you'd better have your computer checked, Alistair. Kathryn Hayes is hale and hearty and very much alive."

Alistair pulled a printout from his attaché case and extended it to Ryder. "Not according to my information."

Ryder waved it away. "Your information is wrong."

"It's never been wrong before."

"Well, it's wrong this time. Damn it, Chambers! Do you have to play this cloak-and-dagger game with everybody?"

"Where you're concerned, Ryder, I must. What if Hayes is an operative sent to uncover your work on the detection of plastic explosives?"

Ryder thought about the stack of notes and mock-ups in the locked room of his Carillon apartment—the room Alistair Chambers had never been allowed access to. As far as Alistair knew, the work existed only in Ryder's head.

"There's nothing to uncover," he lied. "I haven't begun work on the project yet." That, after all, was what their conversation on the jet from St. George had been all about.

"Ryder, Ryder." Alistair ground out his cigarette in the rapidly filling ashtray. "Grant me some intelligence, please. I know what you've done and I know exactly how far you've gotten." Ryder started to protest but Alistair raised his hand. "Spare me. I'm still willing to go along with our agreement but let us at least be honest with one another."

"You son of a bitch," Ryder said, shaking his head in amazement. "How in hell did you know about it?"

"Trade secret."

"You can tell me," Ryder said, unable to suppress his admiration. "My security clearances are top-ranked."

Alistair leaned back and crossed his legs. "Remember that three-faceted multilingual panmedia 900-baud high-frequency transmitter with the decode function in Alpha and Code Z you developed for the Pentagon last year?"

Ryder nodded.

"PAX made a few adjustments and—well, let's simply say that locked doors aren't the deterrent they once were."

"I should have become a plumber," Ryder said sourly. "At least they have privacy."

"You'd hate it," Alistair said. "On call twenty-four hours a day, dealing with emergencies both real and imagined, no time to call your own—"

"Sounds familiar, doesn't it?" What Alistair had been describing was Ryder's life in the organization the past fifteen years.

Alistair acknowledged the similarity. "But, dear boy, very few plumbers have a Rolls-Royce at their disposal or an apartment at the Carillon."

"Not if what I've heard about their hourly rates is true. The plumbers all live at the Trump Tower."

Alistair laughed and, finally, so did Ryder. Both men knew his knowledge of a plumber's wages was limited to hearsay. Ryder's day-to-day reality was vastly different from the day-to-day reality of most Americans.

The limousine exited the FDR Drive and headed crosstown toward the Carillon.

"So now that you know I've started the project," Ryder said, "does that mean our deal is off?" Calm words that hid the rising fear that he'd made himself irreplaceable.

Alistair drew himself up in his seat and looked affronted. "After all the years we've known each other, I'm surprised you would say such a thing, Ryder. If I am anything, I am a man of my word."

"I'm sorry," he said, meeting Alistair's eyes. Alistair had never been anything but totally honest with him. "I must be more tired than I thought."

"You'll have the time and space in which to work, my boy. That I promise you." Alistair paused, his blue eyes searching Ryder's face. "But you are still part of PAX and there are still some things PAX must ask of you."

"Such as?"

"Be careful whom you befriend."

"If you mean Kathryn Hayes, I—"

"Kathryn Hayes, Joanna Stratton, the young man in apartment 3G—you've come too far to make a mistake now."

Ryder tried to make light of Alistair's warning. "I think the Caribbean sun was too much for you, my friend. Next you'll tell me to watch out for my neighbor's Pomeranian—it might have a bug in its flea collar."

"An execrable play on words that I shall endeavor to ignore. Like it or not, you are still part of PAX and all that being part of PAX entails." The limousine lurched to a stop at a red light and Alistair rapped sharply on the divider to caution the driver to pay heed to the job at hand. "Friendship is a risky business for us, Ryder. Our enemies come in many disguises."

The seed Chambers had carefully planted began to take root. A thousand questions Ryder had been ignoring all clamored for attention.

"Damn you," he said quietly to Alistair as the limousine moved forward again. "Damn you."

If Kathryn Hayes were not what she seemed to be, what in hell did that make Joanna Stratton?

THE TWILIGHT ZONE, Joanna thought, looking into the mirror. That was it. Rod Serling had somehow reached out from the Great Beyond and swept her into another dimension of space and time.

Certainly not even her makeup skills could account for the eerie feeling that came over her when she looked at the completed job. All signs of Joanna Stratton had been obliterated. Looking back at her from the mirror was Kathryn Hayes. She'd bet that not even her own mother, would recognize her right now.

The trip to Ranaghan's had been more than worth it. The prefab jowls and flesh-toned latex provided the final finishing touches that had fine-tuned her creation from good to perfect. Benny Ryan and the rest of the crew would be astounded when she worked her magic next week.

She adjusted the cap of gray curls and grinned at her reflection. Maybe she should just show up on the set in her full Kathryn regalia and shock the heck out of them.

The clock in the dining room struck two-fifteen.

"Damn it!"

Joanna leaped to her feet. Cynthia had sent four checks that "must, absolutely *must* be put in the bank by Wednesday afternoon the *latest*, thank you, darling Jo" and Joanna knew what that meant. Cynthia's account was probably overdrawn, the mortgage payment about to bounce higher than a Spalding rubber ball, and it would be up to Joanna to explain to her mother's outraged creditors that some women simply weren't good with numbers.

The hell she would. She grabbed the checks from the lower left-hand desk drawer and stuffed them in her purse with a deposit slip. Cynthia's bank was ten blocks from the Carillon; if Joanna hurried, she could just get there before it closed.

She raced for the elevator, but the door was stuck. No matter how hard she tried to pull it open, it wouldn't budge and Joanna didn't have time to spare. She opened the fire door and raced down the stairs, thankful that her attention to detail hadn't eliminated her trustworthy Reeboks.

THE ELEVATOR DOOR opened as soon as the fire door closed.

"Was that her?" the first man asked.

"Who else? No other old people on this floor."

"What do we do?"

"He said to follow her. We can't do nothing in the building."

"How bad do we hurt her?"

"Bad as we have to."

They took the elevator to the lobby and positioned themselves near the mail room to wait.

RYDER PACED UP AND DOWN the length of his living room. He'd been back in his apartment for less than an hour and already he was climbing the walls—figuratively if not literally.

Alistair had dropped him off after Ryder refused a lunch invitation, and Ryder had been doing his damnedest to pretend he wasn't aching to see Joanna Stratton again. Alistair's warning had unnerved him in a way that surprised him.

Normally Alistair's PAX-instilled brand of righteous paranoia amused him; today it rankled.

All this crap about Kathryn's hands and subversives and who was Joanna Stratton anyway had taken its toll on his temper and he was ready to explode. Pacing a hole in the Berber carpeting wasn't going to solve anything.

What he had to do was go downstairs to the Hayes/Stratton apartment, ring the doorbell and take a good long look at Kathryn Hayes's seventy-seven-year-old hands and be done with it. Then, he intended to ask Joanna out to dinner and, if the fates were with him tonight the way they'd been with him this morning on St. George—well, he'd make damn sure his apartment was bug-proof before he brought Joanna inside.

Five minutes later, he was convinced the fates had deserted him. Joanna wasn't home. Kathryn wasn't home. Even Rosie Callahan next door wasn't home. The tiny Carillon seemed like a high-priced mausoleum and he, the only resident.

Maybe a little fresh air would help, he thought as he took the elevator down to the lobby.

Maybe he'd bump into Joanna.

THE BANK GUARD was just about to lock the front door when Joanna slipped inside.

"You live dangerously, lady," he said, pointing toward the clock near the loan officer's desk. "One minute to spare."

She smiled up at him. "Don't walk as fast as I used to, sonny. Can't get used to making allowances for it."

Actually Joanna had practically flown down Columbus Avenue, causing more than one head to turn at the sight of a septuagenarian attempting to break the four-minute mile. The wait for a teller was minimal, and at a little after three Joanna was headed back to the Carillon, this time at a more leisurely pace.

It was interesting to watch people's reaction to her makeup job. Most walked right by her as if she were a part of the New York scenery, as utilitarian as a wastebasket and just as interesting; however, now and then an elderly man would tip his hat to her and that courtly gesture reminded her of bygone days.

Bygone days? Joanna laughed out loud, causing two teenage girls in puffy down coats to hurry past her. She was beginning to sound like Rosie.

Was age as much the result of how you were treated as how you were feeling?

About halfway to the Carillon Joanna became aware of a strange prickling sensation along the back of her neck that usually accompanied being watched—and watched intently. When she bent over to fix the laces on her right Reebok she noticed a flash of red hair and two males who ducked into the doorway of a health-food restaurant. Was she crazy or could they be Stanley's sleazy new associates?

No matter. Even if they were Stanley's pals, it was none of her business if they decided to sneak out for a beer during working hours. It was the type of loyalty that Stanley deserved.

Besides, it was probably just imagination and hunger playing tricks on her. When she got back to her apartment, she'd fix herself a pot of coffee and dive into the rest of that pecan coffee ring Rosie'd brought over that morning. That should chase any hunger hallucinations away.

However, the odd feeling of being followed wouldn't go away. Twice when she stopped at a Don't Walk sign, she turned slightly and caught a glimpse of red hair in the crowd behind her.

Three blocks away from the Carillon the crowd thinned out and Joanna's uneasiness increased. The footsteps behind her kept pace with the tempo of her walking, and there was no way she could deny that she was being followed. She wanted to stop and turn around, confront the two men. Demand to know why they skulked behind her like thieves. But what if she were wrong?

Innate politeness kept her from making a scene.

Except for the red hair, those two Stanley hired were totally forgettable. She'd be chalked up as another batty old lady, and from what she'd seen while in costume, the elderly had enough to contend with without adding Joanna Stratton to the list.

She crossed to the other side of the street. Her peripheral vision told her they crossed, too. Sweat broke out beneath the gray wig and trickled down the back of her neck.

To hell with propriety. She broke into a trot, weaving in and around strolling pedestrians. The slap of feet hitting the pavement behind her echoed in her head.

She was one block away from the Carillon. The light changed to red. The footsteps were getting closer. She darted into traffic, scraping against the side of a gypsy cab, ignoring the bleating horns and the curses shouted in every language known to humanity.

A few hundred yards, that was all she had to run. Just a few hundred yards and she'd be in the lobby with a doorman and a security system and—

An arm came around her midsection from the back and lifted her off her feet.

"Stop! St—" Her scream was muffled by a dirty rag jammed so far into her mouth that her gag reflex was triggered. She retched violently as she was carried into the alleyway between the Carillon and its sister building, the Dorchester, where the endless rows of metal trash cans were stored.

"You watch the street," the man who held her said to his companion. "I can take care of her."

"Make it fast. We get caught and that's it. We blow the thousand bucks."

She struggled, trying to twist around so she could get a look at their faces, but her assailant kept her facing toward the back of the alley, away from him and his cohort.

"Lay back, Rosie Callahan," he grunted in her ear as she kicked wildly. "Make it easy for both of us."

Chapter Eleven

Good God in heaven, Joanna thought, bile rising into her throat. He was going to rape her. Hundreds of hours of women's self-defense courses hovered just out of reach as her mind went blank with fear.

But it wasn't rape he had in mind. The second his fist slammed into the side of her face, Joanna realized, even through her terror, that something else entirely was going on. This was a systematic, unemotional beating, and the only way she was going to get out of it was to outsmart him.

"Hurry up!" the lookout called from the end of the alleyway. "Don't take all day in there."

"Give me—" his fist connected with her stomach "—another minute."

She closed her eyes and sagged against his arm, feigning unconsciousness. A halo of pain blazed in front of her closed lids as she stealthily reached into her coat pocket for her enormous ring of house keys.

"I'm gettin' the hell out of here, Jimmy," the lookout yelled. "A cab's pullin' up in front of the building."

The sound of his retreating footsteps echoed down the alleyway.

"Then screw your money," Jimmy mumbled, his attention diverted momentarily. "You stupid son of a bitch, I'll keep it all."

This was the moment she'd been waiting for.

Jimmy's head was turned slightly away from her. Joanna tightened her grip on the ring and swung the heavy maze of keys hard into his face.

He screamed with pain, but to her horror, he didn't release his grip.

"You'll pay for that," he said, slapping her across the face. "You'll pay."

Anger replaced fear, and suddenly all those lost hours of self-defense training came back to her as Joanna brought her fist up into the vulnerable spot between his legs. He doubled over instantly. She was about to smash the heel of her hand into the bridge of his nose when he recovered and threw her down to the filth-ridden ground once again.

"This one I'm gonna enjoy," he said, whipping a knife from his pocket. "This one I'm gonna really enjoy."

Fear and rage exploded inside Joanna as she screamed for help. Not fifty feet away pedestrians strolled the city street. Two women peered into the alleyway from the street and hurried past.

Jimmy lunged for her with his knife but she blocked him with her hand. The sting of sharp metal against soft flesh hurt less than the realization that she was about to die and nobody on earth really gave a damn if she did.

RYDER'S LEG HURT like hell, and it was no wonder. For his first day out of the cast, this one had been a killer.

Not only had he dragged himself through a Caribbean jungle, but he'd walked around the Upper West Side, an urban jungle, for two hours and hadn't found a sign of either Joanna Stratton or her grandmother. Finally, after stopping for a slice of pizza at Nino's, he gave in and hailed himself a cab for the ride back to the Carillon.

He'd just paid the driver and when a red-haired guy who looked familiar whizzed past him, almost knocking him down.

"Hey! Watch where you're going!" His leg throbbed ominously. Damn city, he thought as he headed toward the building. The guy didn't even have the decency to break stride a second to see if he'd knocked Ryder flat on his behind.

Who the hell could manage a romance in New York? Dirt. Crime. Crowds. Noise.

He stopped, his hand on the door. The blare of a bus horn mingled with other equally ugly sounds. However, buried beneath the mixture of noises was a high-pitched sound. He stepped back into the center of the sidewalk and listened. There it was again. A scream—and it seemed to be coming from the alley between the Carillon and the Dorchester.

Two young women in identical pin-striped suits hurried past, muttering, "Awful, awful," as he reached the opening to the alley.

He forgot his leg. He forgot his fatigue. He forgot everything when he saw the gleam of the knife and the look of pure terror on Kathryn Hayes's face.

He did what he'd never done before in his fifteen years with PAX: He drew his gun.

JOANNA DIDN'T KNOW what scared her more: the sight of that knife gleaming near her throat or Ryder O'Neal, looking steely-eyed and dangerous, with a gun in his hand. However, it didn't really matter; what mattered was getting out of that alley alive.

"I said, drop that blade."

Jimmy hesitated. Ryder cocked the pistol. Joanna prayed he was a good shot because not more than six inches separated her and her assailant.

"Drop it, you fool," she said to Jimmy. "He'll kill you."

Jimmy stared down at her. "You know him?"

"He's a murderer," she said. "He's on parole."

"Shit. I wasn't bargaining on anything like this."

"I'll count down from ten," Ryder said, his voice more menacing than Joanna could have imagined possible, "and then I'll use you for target practice." He took aim. "Ten...nine...eight..."

"Drop it," Joanna said. "Use your head! Drop it."

Jimmy's hand began to shake. "I don't know—"

"...seven...six..."

"Stanley's money isn't worth it if you're dead," she urged, trying to move away from his grasp and out of the line of fire.

"...five...four..."

He's going to pull that trigger, Joanna thought wildly. Three more seconds and she would be witness to a murder.

"...three...two..."

The blade hit the concrete and the sound echoed between the two tall buildings. Jimmy stood up, hands extended, palms forward, then started to run for the exit. Joanna grabbed for him but got a shred of denim jacket instead.

Ryder was game but his bad leg made giving chase impossible. Jimmy was out of sight before Ryder had gone ten feet.

He limped his way over to Joanna and helped her up.

"Are you all right?"

She looked at the gun in his left hand. "I will be when you put that away."

He slid it back into the holster hidden by his leather jacket. "Effective, isn't it?"

"Very." She shivered. "Thank God you showed up when you did. Another minute and—" The realization of how close she'd come to death hit her full force and she fought a wave of nausea.

"Come on, Kathryn," Ryder said, putting his arm around her. "Let's get you home."

His touch, as he led her back to the Carillon, was gentle. His manner was solicitous and concerned. He spoke to her with genuine affection.

He'd risked his life to help her.

The man was as wonderful as she'd imagined him to be, Joanna thought as the elevator slid up to the ninth floor. Strong and handsome and brave and—

Wait a minute. She was describing a Boy Scout and, unless they'd changed the handbook drastically, very few Boy Scouts carried a revolver beneath their leather jackets.

You fool, she thought. *You pitiful fool.* Last night she had been weaving elaborate fantasies about herself and a man named Ryder O'Neal, dreaming of things she hadn't allowed herself to dream of for years.

Today that same man pulled a gun out of nowhere and it was obvious he damned well knew how to use it. A cold wave of fear, more intense than she'd felt in the alley, spread outward from her gut. What on earth had she gotten herself involved in?

Apparently she wasn't the only one who was a master of disguise.

SHE HADN'T ASKED the question yet, but Ryder knew it was just a matter of time. Any moment Kathryn Hayes would turn to him and say, "What are you doing with a gun?" and he'd be damned if he knew what his answer was going to be.

PAX and his identity had been the farthest things from his mind back there in that alleyway. All he'd been able to think of was saving her life, even if it meant taking her assailant's.

When push came to shove, he was as capable of violence as the next man. For a man who'd spent his adult life trying to come up with ways to combat violence, it was a sobering thought.

Even more sobering was the realization of how close he'd come to blowing his cover altogether.

He'd let down his guard these past few weeks, allowed himself the ultimate luxury of normalcy, reveled in the pleasure of enjoying life without glancing over his shoulder at every turn.

Then he noticed a stray lock of shiny black hair tumbling over Kathryn Hayes's shoulder and he knew Chambers was right.

Real life was the most dangerous game of all.

JOANNA STOOD in the dimly lit hallway and waited while Ryder locked them safely inside her mother's apartment.

"We should call Rosie," she said. "If she's in danger, she needs to know about it."

"We will," he said, putting her keys down on the side table, "but first we have to take care of that hand."

She looked at him blankly. "What?"

"Your hand." He lifted her left hand and she stared at the small cut made by the knife. "It's not serious, but we ought to clean it out and bandage it."

Suddenly she was aware of the throbbing pain that ran along the base of her thumb and she remembered the quick slash of the knife. "My God," she breathed. "I had no idea."

"Adrenaline," he said, leading her into the bathroom. "It does amazing things."

"Evidently." She sat down on the closed toilet seat and watched as he rooted around in Cynthia's well-stocked medicine cabinet for hydrogen peroxide and bandages. "For a moment back there I felt like I could wipe up the alleyway with him."

"You almost did, Kathryn. He's going to have one hell of a black eye."

"Good." She smiled at him. "Better me than Rosie. At least I have youth on my side."

He gave her a funny look as he set things out on the sink, but Joanna was too preoccupied with her dreams of glory to pay much attention.

"A three-year advantage isn't much to crow about," he said, uncapping the peroxide and reaching for her injured hand.

"Well," she said, aware that once again this wasn't the right time for a full confession, "Rosie lies about her age."

"I see."

He flipped her hand over, stroking the smooth white skin with his fingertip as if searching for broken bones. His touch drew her belly into a tight knot and started a painful throbbing in her breasts and between her thighs.

"Does that hurt?"

"A little." The pain, however, had nothing to do with the knife wound.

He drew his finger in the space between thumb and forefinger and she swallowed hard against the obvious symbolism of the gesture.

"The hand is one of those little known erogenous zones," he said, his voice lazy with sensuality. "Thousands of nerve endings all waiting for the right stimulus." His index finger stroked her palm and she felt herself absurdly growing ready for him.

"Ryder," she said weakly. "The peroxide?"

He held her hand over the basin and drizzled the peroxide over it. *He didn't mean anything by that,* she assured herself as he dried her hand and put a Band-Aid over the cut. *Don't go reading things into an innocent statement.* To Ryder, she was seventy-seven-year-old Kathryn Hayes. He didn't know—he couldn't know—how her body ached for him.

"Let me see your other hand."

She kept it firmly on her lap. "There's nothing wrong with my other hand."

"You didn't think there was anything wrong with that hand," he said, pointing to the newly bandaged one. "Come on."

He smiled but the smile reminded her of the way he'd looked in the alley with that gun pointed in her direction. There was something predatory about that smile, something male and savage and dangerous. Something that excited her in a way that should terrify her—if she could just think clearly. Maybe she'd lost more blood than her cut would indicate and was growing light-headed. There had to be some explanation for the strange thoughts that raced through her brain.

Stop acting like a fool, Stratton. Give him your damn hand. He was hardly the kind of man who'd come on to a woman old enough to be his grandmother.

"You have beautiful hands, Kathryn."

"Thank you," she managed.

He drew the palm of his hand over the palm of hers and

his heat burned against her skin. Then he drew his thumb across the fleshy pad at the base of her thumb and her breathing accelerated dangerously. It was the movement of a man well versed in pleasing a woman, a movement that, at the right time and in the right place, would drive her instantly to madness.

"Do you know what this is?" he asked.

She swallowed. "My thumb?"

"Your mount of Venus. The plumper the mount, the higher the degree of sensuality."

Oh, God, she thought. The one possibility she and Holland had never considered: Ryder O'Neal was crazy. Her body, however, paid no attention; it simply burned for him.

"You're a very sensual woman, Kathryn."

She tried to pull her hand away but he held it fast. "Ryder, I really don't think you should be doing this."

He lifted her hand to his lips. "Age doesn't matter," he said, "not when the chemistry is right." His tongue flicked gently across the sensitive flesh of her palm. The spot at the top of her thighs quivered in response. "And it's right with us, isn't it, Kathryn?"

"Yes—I mean, no—oh, God, I don't know *what* I mean." Although Joanna's brain was turning to cotton candy, this time she succeeded in regaining possession of her hand. "Ryder," she said, clenching both hands together on her lap, "things aren't always what they seem."

"To hell with the way things seem to others," he said, totally missing the point. "What we have is strong enough to stand up against the talk."

Holland would never believe this, Joanna thought. Last night in her see-through nightgown, he'd contented himself with fantasy. Today in her iron-gray wig and sensible shoes, he was all over her.

It could start a whole new trend in singles' dressing.

He pulled her into his arms.

"Ryder," she said, as his mouth came closer, "I'm not what you think. I—"

"Shut up."

No five-course meal, no fine champagne ever tasted as wonderful as Ryder O'Neal's mouth on hers. She didn't care if he thought she was Grandma Moses, just as long as this ecstasy never ended. His hands insinuated themselves up her spine, caressing her shoulders and throat, then plunging into her hair.

Wait! The hair he was stroking was removable. She waited for him to let out a yelp of surprise, or storm out of the apartment, or even faint dead away on her finely polished parquet floor.

But he did none of those things. Instead, he jerked her head back until her eyes met his and, in a steely voice she barely recognized, said, "I'll give you ten seconds to explain, Joanna Stratton, and it'd better be good."

Once again he removed that deadly pistol from his shoulder holster but this time he pointed it straight at her heart.

It had been the most extraordinary day of Joanna's life and she did the first thing that came into her head.

She passed out at his feet.

Chapter Twelve

Damn Alistair Chambers and his suspicious, PAX-washed brain.

When Ryder pulled out his gun and watched, horrified, as Joanna crumpled to the floor, he knew in an instant he was totally, absolutely, one hundred percent wrong.

Joanna Stratton wasn't a spy or an operative. She wasn't mixed up in anything, covert or otherwise, that could possibly endanger either Ryder or the organization. She was a makeup artist, exactly as she had said, who got caught in a game of let's-pretend that backfired.

Ryder tossed the gun to the floor just outside the bathroom door and bent over her. With those vivid blue-green eyes of hers closed, she seemed softer, more vulnerable, her fiercely independent nature subdued. Even with that Kathryn Hayes makeup job, the classic loveliness of her bone structure showed through and he knew she would be as beautiful in old age as she was now at the peak of her womanhood.

Her sweater was loose-fitting and dipped to a low V in the back, exposing the smooth white skin of her back. She was totally at his mercy and feelings of extreme tenderness overpowered him. He wasn't used to feeling protective of women his own age.

The nature of his business had kept him on the move all these years, and he'd grown used to taking pleasure where he could, then moving on, living out juvenile fantasies of freewheeling, no-strings relationships where around each corner waited a new woman more beautiful and eager than the last.

When things got too serious there was always the midnight call summoning him away to some other part of the globe. He thought of Valerie and winced. He hadn't been above taking the easy way out.

His feelings for Joanna Stratton were uncharted territory, a strange land he'd once been reluctant to explore.

He wet a towel with cool water and placed it against her brow. She murmured softly and his heart turned over with the strangest combination of sweetness and desire that he'd ever experienced.

It was almost enough to make him forget that when Joanna Stratton finally came to, he was going to have to come up with a damned good reason for pulling a gun on her.

A MAN'S VOICE.

"You weren't supposed to do that."

It seemed to be reaching her from a tremendous distance, taking forever before her brain could interpret the sounds. She felt as if she were suspended in another world.

Then she remembered. Ryder O'Neal. His threat. The gun. Could he have—my God, he shot me! She struggled to sit upright but a wave of dizziness swept over her. Probably from loss of blood.

She opened her eyes. He was leaning over her, looking amazingly distraught for a man who whipped out a pistol the way other men whip out a pack of Marlboros.

"That's better," he said. "You know, you really took all the fun out of it."

"If shooting women is your idea of fun, I'd hate to see you when you're angry." She managed to sit up but a sharp pain in her right arm made her wince. "How bad is it?"

"You'll live."

She was too angry to be afraid of him any longer. "The least you could do is call me a cab so I can go to the emergency room."

"For what?"

"My bullet wound."

His face darkened. "That bastard shot you?"

"No," she said, jabbing him in the chest with her forefinger, "this bastard shot me."

"The hell I did."

"Someone shot me and since you're the only one here with a gun…"

"I couldn't shoot you," he said. "The gun's not even loaded."

"I don't believe you."

He picked up the gun from the floor just outside the bathroom door and opened the chambers. "See? Empty. Nothing. Completely harmless."

"Then why does my shoulder feel like it's been crushed in a Cuisinart?"

"There's a logical explanation," he said, barely concealing a grin. "You hit it on the edge of the sink when you took your dive."

"I didn't take a dive. I had a dizzy spell. A minor one."

He laughed outright. "A dizzy spell? You passed out, Joanna. Cold."

"I've never fainted in my life."

"There's always a first time."

"I refuse to believe it."

"Believe it or not, it happened." He looked at her intently. "You're not pregnant, are you?"

"Bite your tongue!"

"It would be more fun if—"

"Don't finish that sentence, Ryder. Not if you know what's good for you." What on earth was going on? The man tried to kill her and she was indulging in *Moonlighting* banter that Maddie and Dave would covet. *Get hold of yourself, Stratton.*

"The least you could do is help me up from the floor."

"You're right," he said, bending over her. "It is the least I can do."

Before she could react, he swept her up into his arms and started to carry her into the bedroom.

"Oh, no," she said, her face disconcertingly close to his, "not there. The living room will do fine."

"You fainted," he said, his hazel eyes twinkling. "You should be in bed."

"I did not faint, and the sofa will do just fine, thank you."

"I love it when you sound like a schoolmarm," he said. "It goes great with that getup of yours."

Her hands flew to her face and she felt the thick layer of latex of cosmetics. She signaled a left turn. "Back to the bathroom."

He took her back into the bathroom and sat on the edge of the tub while she peeled off the rubbery mask and scrubbed her face clean with lots of soap and warm water.

"The real me," she said, drying her face with a fluffy white towel. "No makeup, no subterfuge, no glamour."

"I like the real you," he said, standing up. "I like everything about you, Joanna Stratton."

The room was large for a bathroom, but not large enough for all that was happening between the two of them. He stepped closer to her and trailed a finger across her left cheek. Joanna's breath drew in sharply.

"You're bruising," he said, his voice angry. "The bastard punched you?"

She gingerly touched the swelling beneath her cheekbone. "Afraid so. I'd forgotten all about it in the excitement."

"You should put some ice on it."

She shook her head. "My skin is too temperamental. Ice breaks the capillaries."

"So does a good left hook."

"I'll be fine," she said, acutely aware of his nearness and her body's reaction to it. The leap from fear to banter to all-encompassing desire was making it hard for her to think. "All I need is some brandy." She raised her arm to turn off the overhead light and yelped. "Damn! Are you sure you didn't shoot me? My left shoulder feels like it's been used for target practice.''

"Let's see.'' He turned her toward the mirror over the sink and slid her loose-fitting jade-green sweater over her shoulder so that both the line of her throat and the swell of her breast were visible.

A mottled bruise was beginning to blossom beneath her collarbone but Joanna had suddenly lost interest in it. Instead her attention was riveted to their reflection in the mirror, to the way his gaze slid over her body like a warm breeze. Gone was the boyish charm, the easygoing, lighthearted man she'd first met.

In his place was the man she'd seen in the alleyway, a hard-edged man whose power easily dominated those around him. He didn't need that gun to be dangerous. He had only to look at Joanna the way he was looking at her now for her to know she didn't have a chance.

She didn't care who he was or what he did or where he would be a year from now. The promise that had been between them from the first moment they met was about to be fulfilled. All she cared about was how it would feel to spend the night in his arms.

A SHOULDER.

In the lexicon of erogenous zones, shoulders ranked pretty low. But when the shoulder belonged to Joanna Stratton, it was a different story altogether.

The sight of Joanna with her oversize jade sweater slipped down over one shoulder was more erotically powerful than anything Ryder had ever encountered. Her silky black hair brushed the top of her collarbone in startling contrast to the pale perfection of her skin. It wasn't hard to imagine how she would feel beneath his hands.

"Well?'' she asked. "Is my shoulder blade bruised?

As he pulled the sweater lower in the back, he tried to gain control of his fantasies. The subtle curve of her waist promised pleasure beyond imagination. "Not that I can see.''

"No bullet wounds?" Her voice was soft, a trifle husky. Her skin was hot and he could smell desire in the air around them.

"No bullet wounds." The urge to bury himself in her warm and willing body was growing harder to deny.

Forcing himself to look away, he met her eyes in their mirrored reflection and in it, found a temptation greater than the one he'd overcome.

For this time he saw not only Joanna in her infinite beauty; he saw them both. He saw the way she looked against him, woman to man. He wanted to surround her, engulf her, lose himself and be found.

There was a rightness to it that went beyond the moment, a rightness that extended into the future and beckoned him forward to a place he'd never been.

There was no force on earth now that could stop what had been set in motion the first moment he looked into her eyes.

THE TENSION in the tiny bathroom was almost unbearable and Joanna knew she had to do something to break the spell. If she stood there one moment longer, she would turn around and offer herself up to him on the alter of desire—an absurd notion, but a heartbeat away from becoming reality.

"Well," she said, her voice strangely husky as she broke eye contact in the mirror, "let's have some brandy."

He said nothing. She could still feel the heat of his gaze. The ache in her body was almost unbearable.

She went to tug her sweater back into place but the touch of his hand on her bare shoulder stopped her.

"Ryder?"

Gently he slid the other side of the sweater down as well until she was bare to the tops of her breasts. A violent surge of passion reared up inside her, causing a path of fire to blaze outward from her belly. He cupped her breasts beneath the silky sweater and her legs trembled so that she had to lean back against him for support.

She watched him as he kissed the side of her throat and the

shoulder that had been hurt in the scuffle. His hazel eyes, dark with desire, never wavered from hers.

"Look," he said, his breath warm and moist against her ear.

Before she could think, he slipped her sweater down to her waist. His hands looked so dark, so large as they spanned her rib cage and inched toward her breasts. There was a rawness about his desire, a fierceness that she'd glimpsed the night before but turned away from. This time there would be no escape.

She wanted none.

The woman in the mirror was a stranger. Her face was flushed; her eyes glittered with excitement. It was the face of a woman ready for her lover; it was a side of herself Joanna had never confronted in quite this way.

She closed her eyes against the wildness building inside her. Her body was opening and flowering, dark and sweet and wet with longing for him.

"No," he said, nipping at the lobe of her ear. "Watch, Joanna. Watch how your body responds to me."

He lifted her breasts in his hands and the fever in his touch matched the fever burning deep inside her body. All boundaries, all rules, all inhibitions vanished.

It was impossible to tell the hunter from the prey, for his need to control matched her need to surrender to that control—just this once.

She placed her hands over his and lightly ran her fingers over her nipples, watching the fire in his eyes snap and blaze. *Don't say anything,* she thought. *Don't analyze, don't worry, don't ask for permission.* She wanted him to make love to her right there, right then, and force everything from her mind but the pursuit of ecstasy.

She didn't want to think. She didn't want to make decisions. She didn't want to worry about tomorrow or the day after.

What was happening was primal, a sensual game of the oldest kind, and for once in her life she wanted to understand how it felt to throw caution to the winds and play with fire.

She didn't even care how badly she got burned.

NOTHING LIKE THIS had ever happened to him before. And, now that it had, Ryder wondered how he'd managed to live without it.

The second he and Joanna shed their clothes—and with it, their everyday selves—he found out that sex for its own sake ran a poor second to what was happening between them.

He couldn't control his powerful response to her nearness—and he didn't want to. Yet, for the first time in his life, he felt unsure with a woman, awkward and uncertain as if he were sixteen years old and just starting to explore the mysteries of sex.

She was tracing the pattern of hair on his chest with the tip of her tongue. His body raged with desire for her, burning hot and hard and ready. Gently he took her hand and brought it to his erection.

Her eyes widened but she smiled and said nothing. Her fingers wrapped around him and her long slow strokes made his stomach knot with the effort to keep from climaxing. His hand slid down over her belly; his fingers tangled in her thatch of silky black hair, then ventured farther until they found the hot, wet, secret spot at the top of her thighs. He parted her gently with his fingers, then let her close around him, her body pulsating to the inner rhythm of life.

She exhaled in a sigh, a long, voluptuous sibilance that he felt throughout his body. Suddenly his own desire receded, replaced by an urgent need to satisfy, to pleasure, to worship.

He dropped to his knees before her. Her woman smell, of heat and sex and life, filled his brain. Clasping her hips with his hands, he showed her all he could not say.

STOP.

He had to stop. Another minute, another instant of this glorious madness and she would shatter into a million pieces.

Surely no one could reach heaven and live to tell about it.

When he dropped to his knees before her and pressed his mouth against her skin, a violent shock of unbridled desire raged through her body and made her cry out. He didn't stop, didn't look up, but she felt his soft laughter against her even-softer flesh and the pleasure he gave her multiplied.

Finally, it was she who could stand no more and she, too, dropped to her knees and told him what she wanted.

Nothing in Joanna's life had prepared her for this. No lover, no fantasy, no midnight dream had come close to what was happening right now, right here, on the shiny parquet floor of her mother's apartment. Not even in the arms of her husband, Eddie, whom she had once loved with the single-minded intensity of the young and innocent, had she ever felt such an overwhelming urge to abandon herself to pleasure.

And when Eddie betrayed her, her need for control had increased until she approached each budding romance with the cool logic of a warrior planning battle strategy.

Logic, however, didn't stand a chance against Ryder O'Neal.

He was everything she didn't want or need: raw and dangerous yet capable of a tenderness that made strong women like Joanna Stratton willingly throw caution to the four winds of fate.

But nothing was forever—she knew that all too well.

Soon her sabbatical would be over and she would follow her career to another city, another assignment, and he would move on to another love. She was old enough and wise enough to know that her dreams of a different life were as fragile as a crystal snowflake.

All she had was this one fleeting moment in paradise and—for once in her life—this one moment was enough.

Chapter Thirteen

While Ryder and Joanna were discovering each other, Alistair Chambers was discovering that drinking alone wasn't nearly as enjoyable as it used to be.

After dropping Ryder off, he headed over to the Russian Tea Room where he dined, oblivious of the celebrities perched in the front booths like so many rare birds on display. He contented himself with a table in the back and vodka.

Lots of vodka.

This whole business with Ryder was taking its toll on him. Last night when Holland Masters had made it crystal clear that she wouldn't mind spending the night with him, Alistair had been too distracted by his worries to take her up on her generous offer.

He shook his head bemusedly. Was old age creeping up on him more quickly than he thought? There'd been a time—and not too long ago, at that—when he would have walked barefoot across fire to bed a woman as lovely as Ms. Masters.

But this whole business with Ryder preyed heavily upon his mind. The boy didn't know what he was getting into, leaping off into real life like this.

The boy needed direction. He needed control. He needed—

Oh, hell. What was the use? If Ryder managed to break away from PAX, Alistair had no doubt he'd be successful in any undertaking he chose to pursue. The world needed genius such as he had to offer; the fact that the genius was slightly unpredictable was a small price to pay.

Alistair drained his vodka. He felt like a father watching his favorite son leave the nest. Ryder was no longer the young boy Alistair had recruited into the organization. He was a grown man who had the right to move on. A grown man who had the right to build a new life.

And that brought Alistair right back to square one.

Out there away from PAX's protection, Ryder was fair game. There were any number of hostile governments eager to tap into a source as limitless as Ryder O'Neal and able to devise some very clever ruses to do it.

Ruses that might include a long-dead old woman like Kathryn Hayes, who could easily get behind Ryder's defenses and find out a hell of a lot more than she had any right to know. It was a fact of life in America that few people took the elderly seriously. A hostile government could have a field day with that.

Old age, he thought as he flagged down Ivan, his Cossack-clad waiter with the Flatbush accent, for another drink. It was a terrible thing. It could set the mind wandering down strange paths and make a man pass up pleasures no sane man would decline.

He glanced at his watch. There was still time to call Holland Masters. Dinner at Le Plaisir would go a long way toward mending fences.

And maybe over dinner, during a lull in the conversation, he could ask a few questions about mysterious—and very much alive—Kathryn Hayes.

IN THE CARILLON, high above the homeward-bound city traffic, Joanna and Ryder were slowly coming down to earth.

Ryder was leaning back against the pillow and Joanna's head rested on his chest. Passions had been banked—for the moment—and the intimacy forged by their lovemaking now strained against the fact that they were virtual strangers.

But, of course, they weren't strangers. Not really. Through

the eyes of Kathryn Hayes, she'd seen a side of him that belied the good-looking, fast-talking exterior. The kindness he'd shown to her while in her Kathryn disguise was as real as the beautiful color of his hazel eyes. Long before he knew Joanna Stratton existed, he'd found time in his life for a woman who could offer him nothing but friendship.

And yet, when she was Joanna, he was everything she'd been avoiding all these years, the one man who could rip past her caution, push past her boundaries, force her to take a good long look at the arid landscape of her life. The one man who could make her fall in love.

No one had ever made her feel this wild, this free. She couldn't stop what was happening between them any more than she could hold back the dawn. What she was feeling for Ryder was as elemental as the wind that blew outside the window and just as impossible to control.

"I wasn't expecting this," she said softly, tracing the pattern of hair on his flat belly.

"I was." He rolled over and drew her into his arms. The pressure of his body against hers was a powerful reminder of the wonders they'd found together. "It was inevitable."

"Nothing's inevitable," she said. "We make our own fate."

His laugh was rueful. "I don't think so, Joanna Stratton, because if we did, we would have run like hell from each other."

"You're very sure of yourself."

"I'm a student of human nature," he said, feathering light kisses along her throat. "I recognize a fellow gypsy when I see one."

Did he also recognize the longing hidden in her heart? The need for the permanence she'd trained herself to believe impossible? How could this intimate stranger see so much and reveal so little?

She leaned on one elbow and looked down into Ryder's beautiful hazel eyes.

"Who are you, Ryder O'Neal?" she asked softly. "Who are you really?"

She had taken off her disguise: Now it was his turn.

TRAPPED.

Joanna Stratton had him trapped.

He either came up with the story of a lifetime or he blew his cover with PAX forever. She deserved the truth—and the thought of leveling with her was tempting—but the consequences for people he cared about were too high. He was still a part of the organization. If he'd learned nothing else from Alistair, he had learned to protect his own.

"I no longer believe you're a spoiled rich kid." She gestured toward the gun on the floor just outside the bedroom door. "What is it you're really all about?"

The idea was on him in a flash. "I'm a private investigator." Thank God for an adolescence spent watching *Mannix* and *Perry Mason*.

She stared at him. "As in *Magnum, P.I.*?"

Not a bad comparison. Selleck had done pretty well with it. "Guilty as charged."

"A private investigator with a broken leg?"

"It happens." He thought about his ungainly tumble from the ski lift. "Occupational hazard."

"No offense, but you don't seem the type."

"None taken." He paused a moment. "What do you mean, I don't seem the type?"

"You're too flashy. Too noticeable." She drew her fingernail lightly across his belly. "Too good-looking to disappear in a crowd."

He felt unduly pleased. "Thank you."

"Don't let it go to your head." He could almost see her donning her emotional armor once again, as if she were afraid that by giving her body, she would give up her self as well. Although she might not believe it, he knew Joanna Stratton was a woman not very likely to lose control of herself or a situation.

"Where does that dapper Englishman I met fit in? Is he your boss?"

Not in this fantasy. "We're partners."

"Fifty-fifty partners?"

"Sixty-forty." He grinned. "My favor."

Joanna kept her eyes trained on his, absorbing every nuance of movement. "So what are you doing here? Are you on a case?"

This was getting ticklish. She had more questions than he had answers. "I've been recuperating," he said, turning on his side and facing her. "Remember the broken leg?"

She looked down at his right leg. "Your cast! It's gone."

"Very observant, Joanna. How else do you think I managed to sweep you off your feet?"

She laughed. "I'd make a lousy detective, wouldn't I?"

"You have other talents."

"We won't discuss those."

"As incredible as those talents are, they're not the ones I meant." He laughed at the look of disappointment on her face. "Your Kathryn Hayes disguise was flawless. You'd be an asset to any agency."

"Is that a job offer?"

He wished it were. Lifetime, guaranteed employment. He started to make a flip remark to cover his deeper feelings when the seed of an idea began to blossom.

For weeks he'd been trying to think of a way to help Rosie Callahan in her battle against the landlord's harassment, but fear of getting too involved made him content himself with installing new locks and giving unsolicited advice.

The viciousness of the attack on Joanna/Kathryn had pulled him into the situation, like it or not. If these bastards were going to play hardball, he was going to give them a game they'd never forget.

"I was only teasing, Ryder," Joanna was saying, moving toward the other side of the bed. "I have more assignments ahead of me than I care to think about. I didn't mean to put you on the spot."

"Maybe I do have a job to offer you."

"I'm listening."

He moved closer. "You'd be helping a friend."

"I'm all in favor of helping friends."

"It might be dangerous."

"I don't mind a touch of danger."

"It might take more than one try."

"I have no other commitments. I can stay here as long as I like."

"The only reward is in doing the job right."

"Money isn't everything."

"We'd be working closely together on this."

The corners of her mouth twitched with a smile. "I've worked with worse."

"Long hours, intense concentration." He paused. "Night work."

She didn't look away. "Whatever the job requires."

"There's one catch, though."

She waited for the punch line.

"You'll have to dress like Rosie Callahan if it's going to succeed."

"Nothing kinky, O'Neal. I draw the line at perversion."

"Nothing kinky. I'm talking about a little undercover work."

Her soft laugh curled itself around his ear. "That's exactly what I was talking about."

"I think you have the wrong idea."

"You're the one who told Kathryn she had a great body, Ryder."

"She does—I mean, you do." He groaned and pushed his hair off his forehead with his forearm. "Damn. I wish I had a tape of everything I said to Kathryn."

"Don't worry," Joanna said. "I can refresh your memory."

"I'm sure you can."

"We're getting off the track. I want to know about this job offer."

He rolled over on his back and pulled her on top of him.

The fact that he could still form a coherent sentence amazed him.

"I think we should consider joining forces."

Joanna said nothing and he realized it sounded like a militaristic proposal of marriage. He'd better rephrase it.

"Rosie is in real danger." He gentle touched the bruise on Joanna's cheek. "You were lucky. Next time, she might not be. I think we can beat Stanley at his own game."

She shifted position and her breasts lightly grazed his chest. This was getting more difficult by the second.

"I'd make a lousy detective." She chuckled. "I'm the one who didn't even realize you'd had your cast removed." She sat up slightly and took a good look at his body. "Or that you have a sunburn in the middle of February."

"Would you believe I have a tanning machine in my apartment?"

"No," she said flatly, "but that's none of my business. I want to know what you think we can do for Rosie."

"We get Rosie to move her plans up a few days and leave for Bert's tomorrow. Then we get you in Rosie Callahan makeup and lure Stanley into thinking Rosie is still in the Carillon. We both know he'll try again. This time we'll be ready for him." In his mind, Ryder had worked out a surveillance system that he would set up in Rosie's apartment, a system that would catch Stanley dead to rights.

Joanna shuddered and Ryder pulled her close, wrapping his arms around her as if he could shield her from the world. For the first time in his life, he wished that were possible.

"Rosie is in real danger, isn't she?" she asked quietly.

"Afraid so. Big bucks are involved here and that means trouble." He pulled the blanket up over both of them. "You've been involved enough, Joanna. You don't need to be in danger."

"No," she said, her voice suddenly strong. "I want to. I've never done anything in my life that was really important. This is my chance and I'll be damned if you take it away from me."

The fierceness of her tone surprised him and he wondered if, perhaps, she too was looking for more than life had previously offered.

"It's not a game, Joanna."

"I know that."

"You might get hurt."

She chuckled grimly. "I already have been."

He met her eyes. "That's not what I mean."

"I know," she said. "But I'm willing to take the chance. All I'm asking of you is the truth. I can handle everything else."

"Brave words. I don't know if you realize how rough things might get."

"I'm not afraid of guns, Ryder. I'm afraid of lies."

Her words found their target and he hoped it didn't show on his face. He'd told her everything he could; more than that was not his to give, even if she was everything he'd ever wanted in a woman.

And when she began to move against him, tempting him, thrilling him, he knew that were he a better man, he would put an end to it right then before she got hurt. Before she discovered that his life was predicated on secrecy and half truths.

But he didn't. He was only human, after all, a descendant of Adam, and prey to all the weaknesses of the flesh.

And just as helpless before the power of love.

"THIS IS GETTING terribly tedious, Alistair." Holland Masters finished the last of her potato skins with caviar and put her fork down. "If you're this fascinated with my friend Joanna, perhaps I should provide her phone number."

"I haven't met your friend Joanna," he pointed out calmly, "I only met her alter ego, Kathryn Hayes."

This was not turning out to be the romantic evening she'd envisioned. "I thought I explained that. Joanna is a makeup artist. She has an assignment next week. Her Kathryn getup was her dress rehearsal."

"And Kathryn Hayes was her late grandmother?"

Holland sighed. "Yes. It's really quite simple, Alistair."

"And who owns the apartment?"

"Joanna's mother."

"Ah, yes. The much-married Cynthia."

"Very good," Holland said, picking up her champagne glass. "There's hope for you yet."

His brilliant blue eyes darkened as he looked across the table at her. Something funny began to happen in the pit of her stomach, something she hadn't felt for quite a while.

"Is there hope for me?" he asked.

She sipped her drink and played for time. "Perhaps."

"The night is young," he said, taking her hand, "and I'm a patient man."

The night was still young and, at that moment, so was she.

RYDER WAS IN A DEEP and dreamless sleep when the high-frequency pulse of the transmitter embedded in his earlobe woke him up.

Damn Alistair Chambers and his sense of timing.

He slipped out of Joanna's bed and headed for the phone in the living room, hoping she wouldn't wake up. He dialed the special phone number, then punched in the four digit code.

"H-Z-3-1-1." Alistair's voice cracked in his ear.

"V-Q-6-4-7." He waited the customary six seconds while the scrambling device took over, preventing the conversation from being taped or monitored.

"Your timing stinks, Chambers. This better be serious."

"It is," Alistair said. "And you are not the only one with previous engagements, my boy. You asked for American problems and you've been granted your wish." Quickly Alistair related a hostage situation in a day-care center in Chicago's inner city where twenty-six children were being held by an escaped prisoner who had rigged all of the windows with explosives. "Cook County asked for the best in the business. It's up to you."

As if there were any doubt. "You know damned well I'll do it."

"That's what I was banking on, son. Be ready in ten minutes."

Ryder hung up the phone, then went back into the bedroom. Joanna was curled around her pillow; her sleek black hair fanned out across her cheek, one leg extended outside of the covers.

There was no time for explanations and no easy explanation he could possibly give. What he wanted more than anything was to lie down beside her and say to hell with Chicago, to hell with PAX, to hell with everything but the wonder he'd found in her arms.

"All I'm asking of you is the truth," she'd said.

Too bad the truth was the one thing he couldn't provide.

Chapter Fourteen

Joanna raised an eyebrow as Holland reached for her third English muffin. "Either you've abandoned your search for perfect thighs or you're in a major depression." She poured them each another cup of coffee. "Which is it?"

"I won't need perfect thighs where I'm going," Holland said in her best Greek tragedienne voice. "The Sisters of the Celibate Poor don't care if you have cellulite. In fact, it's a requirement."

"Sounds serious." The radio had been set to an all-news station and Joanna switched it off. Daily life was depressing enough; she didn't need to hear about grade-school kids in Chicago being held hostage. "Whenever you threaten to join that imaginary convent of yours, I know it means men trouble."

"Not 'men,'" Holland corrected her. "Man. One Alistair Auden Chambers, to be precise."

Joanna, who was still trying to recover her equilibrium after last night's interlude with Ryder O'Neal, kept her eyes on her own English muffin. "What happened?"

"Nothing happened."

"Nothing?"

"You heard me. Nothing. *Nada*. Zero. *Bupkis*."

Joanna started to laugh. *"Bupkis?"*

Holland did her best to stifle a grin. "I got that from Mrs. Weintraub. Descriptive, isn't it?"

"Very." She paused. "What exactly do you mean by, 'nothing happened'?" Joanna knew her flamboyant friend well enough to realize that Holland's interpretation of nothing could be vastly different from her own.

"Exactly that. This time we had a wonderful, romantic, candlelight dinner at Le Plaisir; we took a hansom cab through the park; we necked in the Rolls-Royce on the way back to my apartment; then—"

Joanna raised a hand. "Holland, please. I don't need all the gory details."

"Don't worry," Holland said. "That's just it. There *are* no gory details. We went upstairs and I poured us each some B&B and, boom! He was heading for the door." She slathered some marmalade on her muffin and took a bite. "That's it. I'm over the hill. It's time for the sisterhood."

"Well, I haven't had breakfast yet," Joanna said. "Wait until I finish before you join the sisterhood."

"Who's joining the sisterhood?"

The two women looked up to see Rosie Callahan in the kitchen doorway.

"You're late," Joanna said, motioning her to a chair. "Holland's already gone through half a package of English muffins and there's no end in sight."

"Man trouble," Rosie said, nodding sagely. "For me, it was Hershey bars."

"For me, it's muffins and the convent," Holland muttered darkly. "I've had enough of those faithless creatures. I'm going to put the pleasures of the flesh aside and concentrate on my spirit."

"If you keep eating like that, you won't be able to put the pleasures of the flesh aside with a bulldozer," Joanna said, handing Rosie a cup of tea. "Unless you're planning on auditioning for the lead in *Jumbo*."

In retaliation, Holland smeared another layer of orange marmalade on her muffin.

Rosie shook her head and laughed. "Well, at least Joanna and I aren't planning on forsaking pleasures of the flesh."

Holland instantly looked up and Joanna squirmed in her chair. "I know all about you and Bert, Rosie, but what did you mean by 'we'?"

"I mean our beautiful Joanna and the equally beautiful Ryder O'Neal."

Holland dropped her muffin face down on the tabletop. "Is there something I should know about?"

"No," Joanna snapped, glaring at Rosie Callahan. "Not one damned thing."

"Oh, yes, there is," Rosie continued blithely. "I told Bert that the second Ryder saw Jo in that frilly nightgown, love was in the air."

Holland turned to Joanna, who was slowly sinking beneath the kitchen table. "Your frilly nightgown?"

"A figure of speech," she muttered, cursing Rosie under her breath.

"It wasn't her figures of speech Ryder was staring at," Rosie said with a raucous laugh. "That boy looked at her the way my second husband looked at me when I did the fan dance in Chicago in 1923."

Holland leaned across the kitchen table and tapped Joanna on the wrist with the handle of a butter knife. "Okay, pal," she said. "What gives?"

"What difference does it make?" Joanna countered. "You're above that now. You're joining the Sisters of the Celibate Poor."

"Just because I plan on embracing celibacy doesn't mean I can't appreciate the antics of lesser mortals."

"Well, this lesser mortal has absolutely nothing to say." She shot Rosie another harsh look and the older woman stood up.

"I'd love to stay and chat with you girls, but I have an appointment."

Holland motioned her to sit down again. "Pay no attention to our puritanical friend. Sit back down and have another cup of tea." She grinned wickedly. "I'd love to hear more about Joanna in her nightgown and the big bad Ryder O'Neal."

Rosie cast a look at Joanna. "Somehow I think I've worn out my welcome."

"Why, whatever makes you think that?" said Joanna dryly.

"You don't live seventy-nine years and not acquire some smarts along the way, miss. Besides, I have to get down to Liberty Travel and pick up my tickets. Bert expects me on the nine p.m. flight to Fort Lauderdale."

Things were going more smoothly than Joanna had expected. "Did Ryder see you this morning?" That was probably why he'd been gone when she awoke; he'd been speaking with Rosie about their plans to ensnare Stanley and company.

Rosie slipped on her coat and tucked her purse under her arm. "He spoke to me all right, but how could he see me, Jo? He's in Illinois."

Joanna jumped to her feet. "Illinois!" And she'd thought he'd left early to spare her being the latest bulletin on the Carillon hotline.

"You've heard of it," Holland said. "Right near Indiana."

Rosie was looking a bit bewildered by Joanna's reaction. "He left about two this morning. I—" She hesitated, glancing from Joanna to Holland and back again. "I heard him close the door to your apartment around one-thirty, then that big Rolls-Royce with the handsome English gentleman pulled up and—"

"Your turn," Joanna said, looking at Holland.

"The one in the Harris tweeds?" Holland asked.

Rosie nodded and Holland reached for her fourth English muffin. "They drove off around two o'clock." Rosie shrugged sheepishly. "Insomnia is one of the little perks that come with old age—great if you're as nosy as I am."

Rosie must have realized that her bombshell had upset the two younger women, because she beat a hasty retreat. Joanna walked her to the door.

"I was indiscreet, wasn't I?" Rosie said apologetically.

"A little," Joanna said, giving her a hug, "but so was I." She hadn't realized Ryder's presence in her bed had been quite so public.

Rosie still looked uncomfortable. "He gave me a message for you."

"Oh?" How nice of him, considering he bolted and ran before the light of day.

"He said to check the right pocket of your white satin robe. He left a note."

Joanna blushed to the roots of her shiny black hair.

"Should I give you a piece of advice?" Rosie asked.

"No," Joanna said. "I wish you wouldn't." It was taking all of her self-control to keep from tearing into the bedroom in search of his note.

There was a moment's silence before Rosie spoke again. "Ryder told me what happened yesterday. I appreciate what you two are planning to do for me more than you know." She gently touched the bruise on Joanna's cheek. "Are you certain you want to take the chance?"

"That's the one thing I am certain about, Rosie." After spending the past ten years of her life hiding liver spots and camouflaging crow's-feet, the chance to do something important with her skills was worth any risks she might incur.

"Be careful."

"That's a promise."

Rosie handed Joanna her house keys, and with a wave and a promise to call from Fort Lauderdale she was off.

Now all Joanna had to contend with was Holland Masters. That made Stanley seem like easy pickings.

"The longer you wait, the more questions I'll come up with," Holland called from the kitchen. "You might as well come in and face the music."

The note could wait.

"Ask all the questions you want, Holland," Joanna said as she went back into the room. "I don't have to answer any of them."

Holland, who had switched the news station back on so she could monitor the weather, eyed her over the rim of her coffee cup. "That's a monumentally selfish attitude, Joanna. You realize you alone can answer my most burning question, don't you?"

"No, I don't have Warren Beatty's phone number."

"That's my old most burning question," Holland said. "This is my new one: Are the Messrs. Chambers and O'Neal an item?"

Joanna tried to keep her expression bland while flashes of the night before with Ryder seared her brain. "I can't speak for Mr. Chambers, but Mr. O'Neal is healthy and heterosexual."

"That's what I was afraid of."

Holland's reaction took Joanna by surprise. "I thought that would make you very happy."

"Judging by the sparkle in your eyes, it makes *you* very happy."

"It means there's hope for you and Alistair."

"The hell it does. At least if he was gay, I could understand his lack of interest. The only reason I can come up with now is I don't appeal to him."

"If you didn't appeal to him, why would he take you to Le Cirque and Le Plaisir?"

Holland stood up and struck a few modellike poses. "I'm not exactly chopped liver, thank God. Some men just like being seen with attractive women."

Joanna was used to Holland's blunt assessment of her charms so the immodesty of the statement didn't faze her. "Maybe he's the old-fashioned type. They still exist, you know."

Holland sat back down. "Not in New York, they don't."

"I think you're jumping to conclusions."

"And I think you're incredibly naive. There has to be a reason why two grown men keep disappearing together—in a Rolls, no less—and none of the reasons I come up with are very encouraging."

"Their investigation service could be one of the reasons, Holland."

"What investigation service?"

Ryder hadn't sworn her to secrecy so Joanna felt safe talking about it. "O'Neal and Chambers, Private Investigators, Inc."

Holland started to laugh. "Very funny. Why would a stockbroker and a computer genius sideline as detectives?"

"Stockbroker and computer genius?"

Holland's laugh faded. "Alistair owns his own brokerage firm and Ryder free-lances for him."

"Who told you that?"

"Alistair. Who told you about the detective firm?"

"Ryder."

Holland reached for another English muffin but, mercifully, the package was empty. "One of them is lying," she said, smearing marmalade on a stale piece of Italian bread. "I don't know why, but one of them is definitely lying."

Joanna, who was cynical on the ways of men, could come up with many reasons. "I don't think either one of them is lying, Holland." She raised her hand as Holland started to protest. "I think they both are."

Before Holland could follow up on Joanna's statement, the resonant voice of a newscaster broke into the commercial jingle on the radio.

"We interrupt our normal schedule for this bulletin from Chicago. The hostage situation in Our Lady of Lourdes Grammar School is over. Negotiations broke off just before midnight, Central time, and hopes of freeing the twenty-six children trapped inside the explosive-ridden building had disappeared. However, WINS learned that special forces equipped with the latest in antiterrorist hardware were able to defuse the bombs and allow police to rescue the students safely. Sergeant Peter Fuqua of the rescue squad said—"

Joanna switched off the radio and met Holland's eyes.

"Don't even think it," Holland said. "If there were ever two men least likely to be on a SWAT team, it's Alistair and Ryder." Her laugh was full and throaty. "I mean, really, Joanna! Alistair would need a valet just to carry his Uzi. Why, if he…"

Holland was off and running, but all Joanna could think of was the way Ryder had looked when he turned that gun on her. She knew he was in Chicago, all right.

What she didn't know, however, was exactly which side he was on.

THE SECOND THE DOOR CLOSED behind Holland, Joanna flew to the bedroom for her white satin robe. She stuck her hand in the pocket and found a folded piece of heavy vellum paper, the kind stacked on top of Cynthia's desk. At least he wasn't the kind of man who left Post-It notes attached to your pillow.

"Duty calls," it said in a sprawling script that slanted upward on the right. "I wish it didn't. Ryder."

Brief, to the point, noncommittal. She didn't expect a declaration of love and wouldn't have believed one were it offered, but this carefully worded note irritated her instead. She crumpled it up and tossed it in the wastebasket near her dressing table.

Like a psychedelic dream, things that happened in the darkness changed shape in the daylight until nothing was left but the memory. Maybe what she'd felt—what she thought he'd felt—had been nothing more than lust and the talk of helping Rosie simply the pipe dreams of a man on an adrenaline high.

To hell with men, she thought as she dressed for the studio. Maybe Holland had the right idea after all.

At the moment, the Sisters of the Celibate Poor sounded like the eighties' answer to Club Med.

RYDER WAS FEELING more depressed than a man who had just saved the lives of twenty-six schoolkids had any right to feel. On the flight back from Chicago, Alistair had chatted with the two other PAX members on board, trying to lure Ryder into conversation, but he was having none of it.

The feeling of elation that his success should have brought to him was missing, and he felt curiously flat, like a half-empty champagne bottle after the party was over. He'd wanted to stay with Joanna, to be near her all night, to awaken with her in the morning.

The timing couldn't have been worse. He knew her fears, knew how much it took for her to take a chance on a man who seemed as aimless and useless as he did, and there wasn't a damned thing he could say or do to ease those fears. Not while he was still in PAX.

When this business with Rosie Callahan was over, Ryder would pack up his equipment and get the hell out of the Carillon before he hurt Joanna the way he'd once hurt Valerie.

He might be his father's son, but he wasn't a total bastard. At least, not any longer.

He was just about to knock on Joanna's door when Rosie Callahan's cheerful voice stopped him. "How was Illinois?"

He turned around and looked at Rosie, who was standing in her doorway dressed in a pale blue Chanel suit that, knowing Rosie, was probably the real McCoy.

"Terrific," he said, bending to kiss her cheek. She smelled, appropriately enough, of Chanel No. 5.

"I feel like I should be smuggled out at midnight," she said.

"Don't worry about Stanley," Ryder said. "He's gone to Atlantic City for a few days. Just worry about your assignation with Bert."

"You do have a way with words, honey." Rosie laughed and ushered him into her apartment. Two leather suitcases rested near the door. "I'm waiting for my ride to the airport."

"Did you leave your key with Joanna?"

"That I did." She gave him a sly grin. "I also told her about the note."

He wagged a finger at her. "Don't even think of asking, Rosie."

She feigned dismay. "How could you even think of such a thing, Mr. O'Neal? I am the soul of discretion."

"Not to mention tact," he said, remembering some of her questions that morning. He should never have given that message to Rosie but he knew there wouldn't be time for another phone call and he was desperate to make certain Joanna knew he wasn't a hit-and-run artist.

"Besides," Rosie continued, pouring them each a glass of port, "I don't even have to ask. Joanna blushed redder than my hair used to be and you look altogether too pleased with yourself."

"It's all in your imagination, Rosie," he said easily. "You read too many romantic novels."

"I read mysteries," she countered, "and you're the biggest mystery I've ever encountered, but this time you're out of luck, Ryder. I can read you like a book."

He grinned but said nothing. The doorman buzzed three times and Rosie told him to come up for her bags.

"You two be careful now," she said, kissing Ryder. "I don't want to be reading anything about any accidents here at the Carillon while I'm away. Not on my account."

"Don't worry," he said, walking her out into the hall where the doorman was piling her suitcases onto a hand truck. "This kind of thing is right up my alley."

Rosie's eyes lit up. "Am I finally going to discover just what it is you do for a living?"

They stopped by the elevator and he kissed her on the forehead. "I'm a drifter," he said. "Just a high-priced drifter."

"I'll find out one day, Ryder O'Neal. Mark my words."

Before he could come back with a retort, the elevator doors slid closed and he heard the sweet sound of a woman's voice behind him.

"I'd like to know your secret, too, Ryder O'Neal."

Joanna Stratton watched him from her doorway and the elation he'd searched for in Chicago zeroed in on him in New York.

Chapter Fifteen

Idiotic though it was, Ryder was speechless for a moment. The sight of her, cool and elegant, in the doorway of her mother's apartment sent his entire body into overdrive and he found it difficult to marshal his thoughts.

"Hi," he said, moving toward her. "I missed you, Joanna."

She didn't say anything, simply stepped aside as he went to take her into his arms.

"How was Illinois?" she asked instead, opening the door wider and ushering him into the foyer.

"Cold." He slipped out of his leather jacket and hung it from the doorknob.

He followed her into the living room, enjoying the way her black skirt clung to her hips and thighs. It was hard to believe that this sophisticated, self-possessed woman was the same woman who had lain in his arms the night before. He was beginning to feel as if he'd been dropped back in a parallel universe because this one sure as hell didn't seem the way he remembered.

"Business trip?" she asked as she poured him some brandy.

"Unexpected."

She arched an eyebrow at him as she sat next to him on the couch. "Evidently."

"You got my note, didn't you?"

"You're a man of few words, Ryder."

He tried to remember what exactly he had said in the note but came up blank. "Did I put my foot in my mouth?"

She sipped her own brandy. "Not at all."

The chill in that room was worse than anything he'd found in the Windy City. "Believe me, Joanna, I didn't want to leave." Her eyes were level and grave as she watched him and he resisted the urge to pull her into his arms. "It was an emergency."

"I didn't know private detectives had emergencies."

There was something about the tone of her voice that put him on alert. "Don't you watch *Spenser: For Hire*? Emergency is a P.I.'s middle name."

She was still watching him carefully. "Did it have anything to do with that hostage thing in Chicago?"

Oh God. How in hell could he have been this sloppy? Only a damned fool would have mentioned exactly where he was going. He forced a laugh and prayed it sounded more natural to her ears than to his own. "Do I look like the kind of man who could disarm terrorists?" He concentrated on looking as unthreatening as possible.

"Yes," she said. "You do."

"I'm flattered," he said, although that was the last thing he'd wanted to hear. "I hate to burst your James Bond bubble, but I'm a lowly private eye, Joanna. The most exciting thing I do is track down wayward husbands to the Dew Drop Inn." He prayed she didn't see the beads of perspiration slithering down his right temple.

"Then answer this: Why did Alistair tell Holland he was a stockbroker and you were a computer whiz?"

"That's our standard cover," he said, telling the truth for a change. "He just happens to be more secretive than I am." And a hell of a lot more professional.

"Why is it I still feel you're holding something back?"

"What can I tell you? I guess it's this dishonest face of mine."

"You're probably telling the truth, but—" The look she gave him was too sharp, too assessing for his peace of mind.

"Forget it. Why would you lie about something as unimportant as that? I guess it was just the product of my overactive imagination."

The hell it was. It was the product of a woman with a brain that matched her beauty, a woman who could see through these idiotic lies and reach the heart of the matter in an instant. Not for her the life of half truths and extended trips, of never knowing if it was business or betrayal that kept him away from home.

If there was no escaping his commitment to PAX, then he would make damn sure he escaped Joanna Stratton before things got any more out of hand.

That is, if it weren't already too late.

He was smack in the middle of something more dangerous than bombs, more lethal than bullets, more powerful than ambition. He was falling in love with a woman he could only hurt, a woman who needed dependability and security and all those things a man in his position couldn't possibly give.

All those things he wanted for himself.

Their love was pointless. Useless. Doomed to failure. There was no future at all for them—there never could be. A smart man would turn back and head for higher ground.

But he'd never been that smart—and deep water had never seemed more seductive.

He was a thousand miles away, Joanna thought as she looked at him. Whatever it was that had taken him from her bed last night still exerted a pull on him, drawing him away in spirit if not body.

Sitting there next to him on the couch, it was hard for Joanna to believe they had become lovers less than twenty-four hours ago. Surely several lifetimes had passed between the moment of their first embrace and this endless interlude of uneasy chatter and awkward silences.

If it was a mistake, if what they had begun had already died a merciful death, then say it, damn it. She would still work with him to get the goods on Stanley and he'd never have to know her heart was breaking in the process.

"I think we need a few ground rules," she said, finally. "If we're going to be working together to help Rosie, I think we should—"

Before she could finish her sentence, she was in his arms and whatever it was she was about to say disappeared like a flash of lightning.

"Hello, Joanna," he murmured. "I've missed you."

The feel of his breath soft against the inner curve of her ear sent shivers of pleasure throughout her body. She smoothed a stray lock of hair from his forehead, and, fool that she was, moved closer.

"You missed a wonderful breakfast," she said, trying to ignore the violent physical and emotional effect his nearness was having on her senses. "I make terrific French toast."

"Maybe next time?"

"Who says there'll be a next time?"

It was Ryder's turn to move closer. "There will be," he said. His hands moved to her breasts but stopped just short of touching her. Waves of desire radiated through her lower body and she swayed slightly, her hardened nipples brushing the palms of his hands. Even through her silk blouse, she could feel his heat and she closed her eyes against it.

"How can I count on a next time?" she managed. "Maybe next time you'll be called to Hawaii."

He brought his mouth down on hers, tracing the outline of her lips with the tip of his tongue until she moaned softly. "There'll be a next time," he said. "That's something you can count on."

"We have things to discuss," she managed, pushing him slightly away, a last desperate attempt to regain control. "Rosie...her apartment...oh, God, Ryder..."

He eased her back against the arm of the sofa, his lean, strong body almost covering her own. "Not now," he said, unbuttoning the top button of her shirt and kissing her collarbone and the hollow of her throat. "There will be plenty of time for that later."

This isn't forever, she told herself. This was no more real than the daydreams she entertained, no more substantial than the illusions she created for the camera.

"I'm not looking for permanence," she managed as her hands greedily slipped his sweater over his head, baring his marvelous chest to her eyes. "I never stay in one place very long." One last chance at protecting herself from the inevitable.

"Then we're in agreement." He drew her close until the tips of her breasts grazed the thick mat of dark hair on his chest. The February cold outside was no match for the heat they were generating between them. "I'm a wanderer, too."

"No commitments." She unsnapped his pants and began easing them off his hips.

"No strings." He slid her skirt up over her thighs.

"When it's over, it's over." She lifted her hips so he could slide her panty hose down.

"No guilt." He threw his jeans and briefs on the floor. "No recriminations."

"Just some fond memories." She let her silk blouse drop over the side of the couch.

He grasped her by the waist and positioned her over him. "A modern relationship."

Her mind was spinning somewhere near the ceiling. "Yes," she managed. "No empty promises."

He cupped her buttocks and drew her closer. "The perfect friendship," he said as she eased herself onto him. "No broken hearts."

She opened for him and he slid inside, filling her in a way that made her mind veer out of control. She could no more keep her heart from breaking when this was over than she could stop the wild, sweet madness that enflamed her senses every time he came near.

And, for the first time in years, she didn't care if what they shared lasted four minutes or four days or for eternity.

WHEN THE PHONE RANG at five p.m., Holland knew in her bones that it was Alistair. She picked it up on the third ring, took a deep breath, then did her imitation of an answering machine.

"You have reached the home of Holland Masters. Holland is not available right now. Please leave a message and she will return the call as soon as possible. Beep."

"Beep?" Alistair said. "If you're going to impersonate a machine, Holland, at least learn to do it properly."

"Keep your criticisms to yourself," she said. "Just leave a message."

"An answering machine that talks back. What will American technology come up with next?"

"I don't want to talk to you," she said. "You're in Illinois."

"I'm in New York. I'd like to see you."

"Then watch *As the World Turns* a week from Thursday, channel 2, 1:30 p.m. I play the woman who dented Lisa's Mercedes."

"I'd rather see you, Holland, not a character you play."

She said nothing, just watched traffic rushing by on the street beneath her window. What was it about this man that kept her perpetually off balance?

"I apologize for cutting our last appointment short. It was unavoidable."

"I'm sure it was. Stockbrokers always have midnight emergencies."

"It was a family emergency."

"I thought your family was English."

"My late wife was an American."

"I didn't know you'd ever been married."

"You never asked, Ms. Masters."

"Are there any little Alistairs running around playing croquet someplace?"

"If there were, they'd be in their thirties and more inclined to sit by a pool nursing a gin and tonic."

The sudden image of five baby Alistairs sitting around a

pool in three-piece suits and short pants made Holland laugh out loud.

"Progress," Alistair said. "Your good humor has been restored."

"Lucky for you," she said. "I'm really quite angry with you, Alistair."

"Would dinner at the 21 Club help soothe your soul?"

"It might." Dinner at McDonald's, as long as it was with Alistair Chambers, would soothe her soul but that was the last thing she was about to tell him. Men had enough ammunition in the battle of the sexes. She wasn't about to provide him with any more.

"Say around seven?"

"Say around seven-thirty."

"I'll come by taxi."

"No," she said, grinning. "Come by Rolls-Royce."

His low, amused laugh made her toes tingle. "You're a mercenary woman, Holland Masters. I like that."

Then that makes us even, she thought, *because I like every damned thing about you.*

"One more emergency phone call and our relationship is over," she warned instead.

"Don't worry," he said. "This time, my beautiful lady, there won't be any interruptions at all."

A voluptuous shiver rose from her toes and, for the first time, Holland Masters knew she'd finally met her match.

IF RYDER THOUGHT about it for long—and he was doing his damnedest not to—his capacity for lying was pretty disturbing.

No strings. No commitments. And the ever-popular no broken hearts.

How he'd managed to keep from choking on that hideous string of lies baffled him. He glanced at Joanna, who was sitting cross-legged on the carpet in Rosie's living room, watching as he wired the ceiling for the camera he would be installing behind the enormous lithograph on the far wall. The rush of feelings as she smiled up at him nearly knocked him off the ladder.

Thinking of the past two hours spent in her arms made him alternately euphoric and despondent. She was a wildly passionate woman and he wanted to believe her passion grew out of something greater than lust, more powerful than desire. He wanted to believe that she sensed the same greater force that he did, the same unaccountable yearning toward the future that made the impossibility of the situation that much harder for him to bear.

Love made a man a hell of a lot more vulnerable than he would have thought.

"Hand me the electrical tape," he said, pointing to the end table on her left. "And the needle-nosed pliers."

Joanna grabbed the tape, then sifted through the tools in the pouch next to her. "These?" she asked, holding up a wrench.

"Pliers," he said. "Don't you Manhattanites know anything?"

"Why do you think we have superintendents? We're more concerned with survival on the streets. We let the apartment take care of itself."

He climbed down and grabbed the pliers from the tool kit. "That's how bastards like Stanley get all their power," he said. "You're at their mercy."

She shivered. "Not a pretty thought."

He climbed back up the ladder and she handed him the electrical tape.

"And you're sure this will work?" she asked, holding on to the sides of the ladder while he leaned over to splice two wires together. "This doesn't look like any surveillance system I've ever seen."

He started to laugh. "Forget *Mission Impossible* and *MacGyver*," he said. And PAX. "This is how it's done in the real world."

"Where will you hide the camera?"

He pointed toward a Toulouse-Lautrec print on the window

wall. "The frame is hollow. Rosie said we can carve a small hole in the woodgrain and hide it there."

"Won't that be obvious? I mean, a hole large enough to hold a camera…"

He held his thumb and index finger less than a quarter inch apart. "See this?" She nodded. "That's all the space we need."

"For a movie camera?"

"For a movie camera."

"And you can film the whole room?"

"We can film the whole apartment, Joanna. We'll be adding additional cameras in each room. They'll all be hooked up into this master system." He explained how he would be monitoring the transmissions live from her apartment. She nodded but said nothing. "If you want out, Joanna, it's fine. This system can manage without you."

"The hell it can," she snapped back. "If Stanley comes back from his trip and realizes no one's living here, he won't do a damned thing. I'm just as important to this as you are, O'Neal, so you can take your male superiority and—"

"Whoa!" he said, laughing. "I said, the system can manage without you. The rest of the plan can't."

"Don't try to make amends, Ryder. You put your foot in your mouth and I'm going to make sure it stays there for a while."

The fiercely determined look in her eyes stilled his laughter. "This could be dangerous, Joanna. I want to make certain you realize that."

She met his eyes head-on. "I realize it."

"We already know Stanley plays rough. You might get hurt."

"We've gone over that possibility before."

"You'll be in here by yourself each night. Anything can happen."

"I'm not afraid," she said. "I just want to help Rosie."

"It might be dangerous."

She grinned and snapped her fingers. "Danger is my middle name."

Joanna Stratton, he thought, *where have you been all my life?*

Chapter Sixteen

For the past three days, Ryder and Joanna had been setting the stage to lure Stanley Holt into Rosie's apartment—and their trap. Thanks to a life mask, Joanna's makeup job had been perfected; her costume was ready; Ryder had wired and bugged every square inch of Rosie's apartment.

Tomorrow would be opening night.

Tonight, however, they had other things on their mind.

The lights were low in Ryder's bedroom. The quilt lay in a heap near the foot of the bed; two half-filled glasses of wine rested on the end table near the phone.

The air was heavy with the sweet smell of port and the musky scent of sex, and the only sound in the room was the sound of Ryder O'Neal and Joanna Stratton as they played a game of can-you-top-this.

"The Piazza de Mozzi," Joanna said, her voice muffled by his shoulder.

"Florence," Ryder said, stroking her hair. "Three times." He paused a moment. "Kongens Nytorv."

"That's easy. Copenhagen. The statue of Christian V is there."

"Memorizing the Michelin Guide doesn't count," he said. "Firsthand experience only."

She poked him in the belly with her forefinger. "My mother's second husband had a home there. I spent two summers with them."

He tilted her face toward his. "No one place to call home?"

Something about the look in his eyes made her breath catch. "Oh, you know my story," she said, struggling to keep her tone light and breezy. The fact that she had shared so much of her life with him—in such a short period of time—still amazed her. "Always on the move. Cynthia's apartment was the closest I ever got to having a home. I guess I come from gypsy stock."

"Not me," he said, drawing her closer to his side. "My family is rooted in Nebraska soil."

Joanna's interest was immediately piqued. This was the first time Ryder had even hinted at having a family. She was beginning to think he sprang from the same mysterious source as his pal—and Holland's—Alistair Chambers.

"If they're so firmly rooted," she said, "how did you end up as a rolling stone?"

"I take after my father. He liked to get around."

In the gathering darkness, she couldn't see his face, but the tone of his voice told her he had said more than he'd planned. She remembered the night the story of Eddie's death had leaped, unbidden, to her lips; she remembered the way it had felt to finally rid herself of the truth.

"I'm a good listener," she said.

"Not much to listen to," he said, his mouth pressed against her hair. "My old man wasn't cut out for nine to five or a house filled with kids and wet sneakers. He took the next train out when I turned nine."

What had happened to his story of being to the manor born? "Hard to imagine a mansion filled with wet sneakers," she said. "What did the help think?"

He raised up on one elbow and she caught a glimpse of his face in the shadowy light. "No mansion, Joanna. Just a frame house on the corner of a rundown, middle-class street in Omaha, Nebraska."

His story about being one of the privileged classes had never quite jibed with the street-tough look in his eyes. "You had me fooled, Ryder.''

"I know," he said softly. "I almost had myself fooled."

THE WORDS WERE OUT before he could censor them, and yet once he said them he was glad. He was getting tired of games and they were running out of time.

She gestured toward the opulent apartment around them. "This is a far cry from Omaha. How did you make the leap?"

How the hell was he going to balance his need to open up to her with his responsibility to PAX? "I met Alistair when I was nineteen," he said. "He opened up a whole new world to me." True enough.

"Computers?"

"Among other things."

"I have a million questions," she said.

He pulled her closer to him in the darkness. "I don't have a hell of a lot of answers, Joanna."

"Sometimes you scare me," she whispered. "Every time I think I understand who you are, I realize I don't know anything at all about you."

"You know everything that matters," he said, moving his lips against her. "You know how I feel."

"I don't ask for promises, Ryder. I don't believe in them."

"You can believe in me," he said, fool that he was. "You can believe I'll never hurt you." For a moment, he was about to forget about PAX and commitments that went far beyond his pitiful need for normalcy.

"I want to believe," she said softly. "This time I want to believe."

More than anything, so did he.

LAST NIGHT HAD BROUGHT them closer; there was no doubt about it. Somehow the darkness and the wine and the accumulated pleasures found in working together had combined to knock down their individual barriers and underscore the seriousness of their growing—yet ultimately doomed—relationship.

Working with him as he set up the equipment there in Rosie's apartment, spending hour after hour talking and laughing while they worked—and while they made love—made Joanna realize just how cautious and cynical she'd allowed herself to become.

How could she have forgotten how splendid togetherness could be? Even the fact that happily-ever-after wasn't in the cards for them wasn't enough to dilute Joanna's joy. For the first time in years, she felt as if what she was doing mattered, that instead of catering to vanity and America's slavish devotion to beauty, she was actually using her talents for a greater purpose.

Combining her skills with Ryder's in order to help Rosie and the other elderly tenants in the Carillon was enough to make her overlook the danger she was in and savor every moment. She wondered how she could ever return to the superficial world of Hollywood illusion and Broadway glitter.

The blend of personal happiness and professional satisfaction she'd found these past few weeks was more than she'd ever dreamed.

And so was Ryder O'Neal. The fact that he seemed to enjoy her company as much when she was in full Rosie Callahan makeup as he did when she was herself, naked and willing and wrapped in his arms, was enough to win her cautious heart.

It was hard not to fall in love with a man like that, even if he did have the alarming habit of making telephone calls at odd hours of the night, muttering chemical formulae in his sleep and keeping two out of eight rooms in his apartment dead-bolted shut.

She adjusted the grayish-red wig on her head and arranged the curls on her forehead. Lovesickness, however, didn't keep her from wondering what lay behind those locked doors.

Maybe private eyes stockpiled guns. Maybe he had filing cabinets crammed with photos of celebrities in compromising positions. Maybe his walls were lined with electronic bugging equipment that cost more than three Mercedes and a Porsche put together. Maybe— Ryder tapped on the door to his bedroom where she had been changing. "Come on, Stratton. I want you out and visible before Stanley finishes his rounds."

Joanna pushed her crazy notions out of her mind and stood up. This was it, then, her first time out as Rosie Callahan's double. Ryder's first impression would tell her everything.

"Come on in," she called. "I'm all ready."

He opened the door. "It's about time. If we don't get—" He stopped dead in his tracks and stared at her. "Son of a bitch."

She glanced at her reflection in the mirror. "Is that good or bad?"

He took her by the arm and led her over to the window where the noonday sun hit her full in the face.

"It's unbelievable," he said, lightly touching her forehead, her cheek. "If I didn't know better, I'd swear you were Rosie Callahan."

Joanna was always confident in her work, so the surge of pleasure that Ryder's compliment afforded her came as a surprise. "Now let's hope Stanley falls for it."

She followed Ryder out into the living room where he handed her one of Rosie's voluminous fur coats.

"Okay," he said, leaning against the black lacquered table near the window, "let's run through it one more time."

"If Stanley is working on the broken stair near the mail room, I'm to pull my shopping cart by him, making sure he gets a good look at me."

"No matter what Stanley says, keep your mouth shut."

"That's not in character. If there's one thing you can be sure of, it's that Rosie Callahan never keeps her mouth shut."

"This isn't the Actors' Studio, Joanna, and you're not Rosie Callahan. Let Pacino worry about the Method—you just worry about getting to the store and back without tipping our hand."

"I'll try to manage that." Her tone was frosty.

"Sorry," he said. "But we only have a few more days to get the goods on him." Once Rosie was back, they would concentrate more on keeping Stanley out, not luring him in.

"He's going to try something today, Ryder. I can feel it. Stanley's a shrewd man; after that mess in the alleyway with his two pals, he's not about to take any unnecessary chances." The thought of catching that bastard in the act made her adrenaline surge, and she poked Ryder in the chest for emphasis. "He's been watching and waiting and, you mark my words, he's ready to strike."

Adding another layer of black mascara to a starlet's eyelashes had never provided excitement to match this.

"This is really getting to you, isn't it, Joanna?" His hazel eyes, rich with gold and green highlights, sparkled in the sun.

"I was born to this life, Ryder. I couldn't wait to get back from that damned studio and get to work." She gave him a hug, then laughed as he sneezed from Rosie's flowery perfume. "Do you think the CIA is looking for a few good women?"

"I wouldn't know. It's been a while since the CIA and I have been on intimate terms."

"Just as well. I can't afford encumbrances. Spies have to travel light." She slipped on Rosie's coat and draped a scarf around her throat. "Sorry, Ryder, but from here on in, my clandestine activities will have to be top secret." She grinned as she headed toward the door. "You understand, don't you?"

RYDER UNDERSTOOD, all right. He understood too damned well.

Joanna had no idea how close she'd come to the basic conflict of his existence these past few months: Trying to figure out how to balance a real life with a professional life that was predicated on subversion and secrecy.

In the scheme of things, what he was doing for Rosie Callahan was not about to change the world. Governments wouldn't rise or fall depending on the outcome; global safety wouldn't be ensured for future generations.

All that would happen was one elderly woman would secure the right to a peaceful life in her own apartment.

Not the stuff of which headlines are made.

But the pleasure Ryder felt working side by side with Joanna Stratton on something they both believed important, surpassed the adrenaline rush of excitement he got out in the field. For a woman with no experience in this kind of work, Joanna was enthusiastic, fearless and, most important, exceptionally talented.

He'd seen the life mask of Rosie Callahan from which she'd patterned her latex-and-foam disguise. He'd watched as she applied the potions and paints and shadows that gave it life and dimension. He's stared as she turned into Rosie Callahan right before his eyes.

He also knew the type of courage it took for her to place herself in jeopardy as she was doing. Stanley was capable of violence; her experience in the alleyway proved that. He would never forget the sight of Joanna—in her Kathryn disguise—trading punches with that punk Stanley had hired to rough up Rosie.

What wouldn't it be like to work side by side with a woman like that, a woman who gave as good as she got, who had more courage in her little finger than most men had when they packed an Uzi in their briefcase. To be able to share the ins and outs of a profession understood by no one but those already in it—

"Forget it," he said out loud. He wasn't one for impossible dreams and the dream of a future with Joanna Stratton seemed the most impossible one of all. She needed security and honesty and stability, all the things he couldn't possibly give.

In a few weeks when they each moved on to the next thing in their lives, he'd look back on this and take bittersweet satisfaction from the fact that, at least once in his life, he did the right thing.

Alistair had been right all along. PAX was in his blood and in his bones; his work with them was the right and natural extension of the skills with which he'd been blessed. To turn away from what he could accomplish with the organization was to turn away from the one thing he'd always been proud of: his involvement with protecting the innocent.

Even during his period of wild self-indulgence when he cavalierly dismissed Valerie's love, his work had remained constant, the one truly valuable thing he was capable of.

He knew that now.

But it wasn't enough. He wanted more. He wanted everything else good that life had to offer—and he wanted to share all of it with Joanna Stratton.

He'd make no impossible promises, he'd raise no false hopes—especially not his own. What he did to Valerie Parker, he would never do to Joanna.

If anyone's heart broke, let it be his.

THE TENSION WAS DRIVING Joanna out of her mind.

"How do you do it?" she said as Ryder fiddled with the contrast on one of the monitors providing a full view of Rosie's apartment. "I can't take much more of this."

Two hours had gone by since she had slipped back into Ryder's apartment via a seldom used delivery entrance, taken off her Rosie disguise and gone up to her mother's place. Not once had Ryder budged from his spot in front of the five monitors set up on her mother's prize rosewood table.

"It's only four o'clock," Ryder said, leaning back in his seat and grabbing for another slice of pizza. "Stanley knows Rosie never gets home before six."

"All the more reason for him to do something now. Why risk getting caught?"

"Still think detective work is glamorous?" He offered her a bite of his pepperoni but she shook her head.

"How can you think of food right now? We should be coming up with an alternative plan."

"We have the best plan available right now," he said in a tone so reasonable she wanted to smack him over the head with the empty pizza carton. "We've set the trap and now all we have to do is wait."

Joanna, however, was sick of waiting. She wanted action. "Maybe we need to change the bait. I could get back into costume and—"

"Forget it," Ryder said. "We're not going to run the risk of another mugging. Let's give this a shot, Joanna. Then we'll start talking of alternatives."

"Maybe you have the patience to sit there staring at a TV screen all night, but I don't. If something doesn't happen soon, I'll just go downstairs to Stanley's apartment and—"

"Shh!" Ryder grabbed her wrist and pulled her near him. "Look."

He directed her attention to the first monitor that covered the foyer of Rosie's apartment. Unbelievably, Joanna heard the sound of a key in the lock and she watched as the door swung open and Stanley Holt stepped inside.

A whoop of excitement rose up from nowhere and she battled to keep it trapped behind her teeth. Stanley was just on the other side of the wall; if she gave things away now, all their work would be in vain.

"My God," she whispered as Stanley double-locked the door behind him from the inside. "Look how cool he is."

"Practice," Ryder said quietly. "The bastard's had a lot of practice."

No doubt.

As Joanna watched in fascination, Stanley strolled casually through the foyer and into the kitchen where he first helped himself to a banana, then polished off the rest of a box of Godiva chocolates Rosie'd been storing in her refrigerator.

"That proves Rosie's story about the missing steaks," Ryder said, jotting something down in a small notebook.

Watching Stanley, so calm, so casual, as he violated Rosie's privacy, put Joanna into a rage. She had to jam her fists into her pants pockets to keep from punching a hole in the adjoining wall as she followed his progress through Rosie's apartment.

Next to her, Ryder took a gulp of Pepsi to wash down the pizza. Food and drink were the last things on Joanna's mind. How on earth did he manage to stay as cool and collected as Stanley Holt?

"There he goes," Ryder said, his voice low. "He's heading into the bedroom."

"Probably looking for more girdles," Joanna muttered, ashamed she hadn't believed Rosie's story the first time around. She was as guilty of ageism as anyone else and the thought rankled.

This time, however, Stanley wasn't on a girdle hunt. Joanna watched as he first pulled out Rosie's bureau drawers and replaced them in reverse order. Next he emptied her closet of shoes and hid them beneath the bed, in the vanity beneath the bathroom sink, behind drapes and chairs and in the hall closet.

Small things—insignificant things to someone else. But to an elderly person aware of the many ways age chooses to manifest itself, these things could be devastating.

Joanna watched quietly, so intent upon the screen that she felt as if she were being drawn into it. Stanley turned to leave, then apparently thought better of it. For a second he faced the camera directly—his lumbering frame poised in the doorway—and Joanna clutched at Ryder's shoulder.

"He knows," she hissed. "Ryder! He knows."

"He doesn't know anything," Ryder said, turning the audio up until they could actually hear Stanley's rapid breathing. "The bastard doesn't know a damn thing."

Without the false good nature and the servile smile, the real Stanley Holt faced the hidden camera.

After what seemed like endless moments, he walked straight over to the bureau, pulled open the top drawer and took Rosie's favorite thirty-six inch string of pearls, the ones from her third husband, Sir Reggie Pembroke, the dissipated landowner from Sussex who had followed Rosie around the world until he convinced her to marry him.

Joanna was ready to leap into action. "Come on," she said, heading for the door. "We can't let him get away with that."

Ryder left his position in front of the monitors for the first time in hours and grabbed her before she could leave the room. "You're not going anyplace."

She tried to yank her arm away from him but his grip was

stronger than she was. "The hell I'm not. If you think I'm going to stand here and watch him steal Rosie's pearls—"

"You're not going to stand anywhere," Ryder said. "You're going to sit down until I tell you to get up."

The punch she'd been withholding for hours finally broke free and landed smack in the middle of Ryder's flat, hard belly.

"The least you could do is groan," she said as he unceremoniously pushed her down into the chair near the monitors.

"You're lucky I didn't belt you back. You should be grateful for my self-control."

She watched, horrified, as Stanley pocketed the string of pearls, then ambled back into the kitchen where he polished off the last of the bananas.

"Call 911," she said, pointing at the screen. "We can nail him right now!"

Ryder said nothing. They both watched as Stanley wandered through the dining room, the living room, then finally back to the foyer. He unlocked the door and, to Joanna's dismay, let himself out of Rosie's apartment without a backward glance.

"It's not too late," she said. "We could grab him before he gets on the elevator."

Ryder shut down the monitors and stretched.

"Let him go," Ryder said. "I know a better way."

"There is no better way. Now that we have proof, the police have to listen to us."

"Think, Joanna." Ryder leaned over her. "Think about what would happen to Rosie the second they let Stanley out on bail."

Joanna pushed back her chair and stood up to face Ryder. "Think about what will happen to Rosie if we don't try to stop him." She gestured toward the array of electronics equipment scattered around. "Why did we bother with any of this garbage if we were going to let him off scot-free?"

"He's not going to get off scot-free," Ryder said. "I just know a better way—a way that won't backfire on Rosie."

"What?" she demanded, stepping closer. "What way?"

"Sorry," he said, shrugging his broad shoulders and flashing her a smile. "You'll just have to trust me on this one."

At that moment, sailing the Atlantic in her bathtub would be easier than trusting Ryder O'Neal.

"Sorry," I said, shrugging his broad shoulders and then... [faded illegible text] ... help her a little... "God you had to go over the crystal care... At this moment any case is whether it... might... would be easier. Can't stand thought of Beck."

Chapter Seventeen

From the start Ryder had known he couldn't turn the films over to the police the way Joanna expected. There would be questions to answer, identification to cough up, explanations necessary for the sophistication and scope of the equipment stashed in his apartment.

The thought of anyone messing with his work on detecting plastic explosives was enough to make him break out in a cold sweat.

There had to be a better way and finally he'd come up with it.

PAX.

Just once, PAX could forget about global terrorists and international intrigue and try something on a smaller scale, something that would help a few people in a medium-size building in New York City to live a better life.

A simple request. And for PAX, an easy one to fill.

Nothing fancy. Nothing earthshaking. Alistair would make a few phone calls and Ryder would deliver the films to the proper hands and this problem with Stanley Holt would be a thing of the past. Rosie and the other elderly residents of the Carillon would be able to live their lives free from harassment and danger.

That was the very least an American could expect in his or her golden years.

Besides, it wouldn't hurt the guys in the organization to be reminded that sooner or later even James Bond grew old, and a new James Bond, younger and stronger and more virile, waited to take his place.

It just might keep them on their toes.

Of course, the problem of Joanna still remained.

"Why are you looking at me like that?" he asked, although he damned well knew the answer. "Don't you believe I'll take care of things?"

She had the most disconcerting way of maintaining eye contact and it took a hell of a lot of effort to keep from glancing away. "I'd feel better if the police were taking care of things."

"Thanks for the vote of confidence."

"You must admit you're mysterious, Ryder—those stories about being a private investigator, those locked rooms in your apartment, Alistair's swearing that you're a computer whiz. You can't blame me for being uncertain."

"You have my word, Joanna. Rosie won't have any more trouble, but you'll just have to trust me on this."

Those blue-green eyes of hers seemed to see right into his heart and she nodded. "I will," she said softly. "God knows why, but I will."

If the situation were reversed, he knew damned well he'd be dialing 911 before he drew his next breath.

He stepped closer to her, desire beginning to warm his blood, heighten his senses, charge his dreams.

"There's no future to this," he said as she moved into his arms. "We both know that, don't we?"

Her fingers trailed up his rib cage. "Life is too unpredictable." Her lips were soft against his neck. "Today is all that matters."

"Tomorrow you could be in Timbuktu," he said, his hands slipping over the curves of her hips and waist. "Or back in Hollywood."

"And you could be chasing wandering wives in Alaska."

"A future would be impossible for us."

She nodded. "Impossible."

He found her lips with his own and her scent and taste and

feel inspired a thousand fantasies. He would have sold his soul if one of those thousand fantasies contained the key to a happy ending, but unfortunately that happy ending seemed as impossible as before.

"I shouldn't trust you," she said as they moved toward the bedroom in a fog of love and desire. "Nothing about you makes any sense."

The words he'd held back refused to be contained any longer. "I love you, Joanna," he said, meeting her eyes and letting her slip behind his barriers. "I love you more than I thought possible. That's the only thing I can tell you."

For the first time since he'd known her, that relentless gaze of hers wavered, and when she looked away he knew—PAX or not—that he didn't stand a chance.

WORDS, Joanna told herself as she tried to regain her composure. *They're just words.* She was old enough and experienced enough to know that what was said in the heat of passion was often forgotten once that passion cooled.

Ryder's words, beautiful though they were, couldn't change the reality of their situation and she would be wise to keep that thought firmly in mind.

But, of course, it was difficult to think clearly when the man you love is sweeping you off to bed.

And it was hard to make sense of his words when his hands and mouth and body were telling you secrets and showing you miracles you had never imagined.

And it was impossible to keep from hoping that maybe—just maybe—he would turn out to be a high school teacher with a steady job, paid vacation and a great imagination.

FIREWORKS.

Skyrockets.

Waves crashing against the shore.

Every single cliché devised by incurable moviemaking romantics to describe the main event fell pitifully short of Holland Masters's first night in the arms of Alistair Chambers.

They were lying in his enormous bed. The only illumination in the room was the reflection of the lights in Central Park and the two glowing red dots from those wonderfully decadent European cigarettes Alistair carried and Holland adored.

It was a scene straight out of *The Way We Were*, where the two mismatched lovers find their brief moment of bliss.

And, of course, Holland got top billing.

"More cognac?" he asked.

"Love it." She extended her glass and he poured a generous amount into it. Even the cognac was exquisite. "I must say you were worth the wait, Alistair."

His chuckle made his chest rumble beneath her head. "As were you, Holland. When you—" His words were low and intimate and so excitingly explicit that she spilled some brandy on her breasts.

"Oh, damn!" She sat up, pushing the Pratesi sheets down and putting her glass on the nightstand. "Get me some water, Alistair, please. I don't want to ruin your pricey linens."

He didn't reach for the water or run for a towel or do anything Holland would have imagined. Instead, he flipped her onto her back and slowly—wildly—proceeded to lick the wine from her body.

No struggle or coy protests from Holland Masters. Those were the tactics of naive young girls who hadn't spent forty-two years searching for the perfect lover.

Nineteen-year-old cuties believe a better man is always right around the corner. By the time you're forty-two, you've turned enough corners to know when it's time to settle down.

Alistair Chambers didn't know it yet, but he would soon enough. She moaned as he did something particularly inventive. Ah, yes—soon enough.

She wasn't about to let him get away.

RYDER WAS TRUE to his word.

Before Rosie returned from her rendezvous with Bert Hig-

gins, Stanley had been unceremoniously replaced by the Vin-
cenzos, a husband and wife team, and the Carillon management placed under state investigation.

No police showed up. No late-night visits from strange char-
acters. No way Joanna could tell how Ryder had achieved this
particular miracle.

In fact, it was a good thing she was occupied at the studio
the next week, because she might have given way to temptation and picked the locks to his secret rooms and rummaged
through his belongings until she came upon the key to what
made him tick.

The first chance she had to talk about this with anyone was
four nights after their successful filming of Stanley raiding
Rosie's apartment. Holland finally had an evening free, and
since Ryder was busy Joanna had her friend over for dinner.

"My God!" Joanna said as Holland slipped out of her coat
and sat down in the living room. "Tell me your secret. You're
absolutely glowing."

Not once in the ten years of their friendship had Holland
ever looked more beautiful.

"I'm in love," Holland said, smiling broadly. "It's better
than a weekend with Elizabeth Arden."

So far, love had given Joanna sleepless nights and permanent circles under her eyes. She perched on the arm of the
sofa and stared at her friend. "Alistair?"

The twinkle in Holland's eyes gave her away. "Who else?
You wouldn't believe the super man hidden away beneath
those Harris tweeds. Why, he—"

"Oh, no, you don't! If you start telling me his sexual secrets, I'll never be able to look the man in the face."

Holland sniffed indignantly. "I certainly don't intend to
share the intimate details of the man I love, Joanna. How
crass."

Before that moment, Holland had thought nothing of dis-
cussing everything from the size of a man's jockey shorts to
what he liked to mumble in the throes of passion.

"It must be serious," Joanna said, shocked. "When? How? Last time I heard, you hadn't even made it to the first kiss."

"Let's just say things have progressed nicely."

"Nicely? What do you mean 'nicely'?" Joanna was finding the new, discreet Holland Masters a bit hard to take. "You look like Scarlett O'Hara after Rhett swept her up the stairs. What's going on?"

"We're getting married."

"What?" Joanna leaped off the arm of the sofa in excitement and grabbed Holland in a bear hug. "I can't believe it! When? Can I be your maid of honor? Where's your ring? He must be thrilled."

"He will be." Holland smoothed her hair back in place and smiled serenely.

Joanna's excitement deflated like a punctured inner tube. "You're not engaged?"

"Not officially."

"But he has brought up the subject?"

"Not in so many words."

"Well, what words did he use?"

"You're very nosy, Joanna. I never realized that before."

"That's because you were too busy baring your sex life to me before. I never had a chance to be nosy." She sat down on the cocktail table, right in front of her friend. "Are you getting married or aren't you?"

"I am," Holland said. "I just haven't told Alistair yet."

Joanna groaned. "I thought so."

"He'll be surprised," Holland said, inspecting the manicure on her left ring finger, "and he'll kick up a bit of a British fuss, but I'm certain he'll see the wisdom of it."

Holland certainly did.

"So why aren't you with Sir Wonderful tonight?" Joanna asked. "Are you granting him time off for good behavior?"

"Listen, Joanna, if I had my way, I'd be having my way with him even as we speak. It just so happens he was called away on business."

An alarm tripped deep in the pit of Joanna's stomach. "Was he called away around seven this morning?"

Holland shot her a look. "Have you added voyeurism to your many talents?"

"Don't be evasive, Holland. This is important."

"Yes, he was," her friend said. "Not that it's any of your business."

"It is my business. Ryder was called away, too."

Holland shrugged. "What's so unusual about that? They're business partners. It stands to reason that whatever affects one partner, affects the other."

"Stockbrokers don't get called away at seven in the morning, Holland."

"Maybe he's still on London time." Joanna made a face and Holland shrugged. "All right, so maybe that stockbroker story was a bit farfetched. So, they're private investigators, instead. What difference does it make?"

"Don't you think a relationship should be built on honesty?"

"There's plenty of time for honesty later on," Holland, who had never been married, said. "Once the fireworks have died down, then we can get around to baring our souls."

"You don't care what he does for a living?"

"What is this?" Holland countered, sounding annoyed. "Twenty questions? What's wrong with you, Joanna?"

"Nothing's wrong with me," she lied. "I just think we should both face the issue squarely."

"Do you know something I should know?"

Joanna shook her head. That was the problem. A dozen suspicions whirled around inside her head but she was loath to give voice to any of them. Ryder owed her no explanations for his behavior. Hadn't they made it a point to declare their mutual independence? Hadn't the subject of the future been relegated to some far corner of their minds, never to be disturbed?

"Ignore me," Joanna said finally. "This is what happens when you grow up on a steady diet of Nancy Drew books."

"You're not keeping secrets from me?"

"No secrets." Only questions and Joanna would spare her friend those.

Ryder O'Neal was the only one who could answer them, and at the moment he wasn't talking.

"Come on," Joanna said, standing up. "Let's adjourn to the dining room. I did promise you a meal, didn't I?"

"That you did." Holland's lovely face relaxed and Joanna's heart went out to her.

Maybe she was being too suspicious, her feelings colored by her disastrous marriage and her mother's peculiar brand of serial monogamy. If Holland Masters, world-class cynic, could bend with the winds of change, why couldn't Joanna?

When Ryder came back, she was going to give it her best shot.

THE WIND from the North Atlantic howled around the small cottage and shook the windows in their frames. Enormous pewter-gray clouds hung low over the rocky coastline and it wasn't hard for Ryder to understand how legend had it that the Isles of Scilly, off the southwestern coast of Cornwall, England, were the mountain peaks of the lost island of Atlantis.

The rough beauty of the land spoke of Celtic legends and ancient glories, of druids and demons and things that went bump in the night. It was a place of otherworldly wonder and, now, a place of threat and danger.

Ryder, Alistair and six other PAX operatives were on tiny St. Margaret, one of the Isles of Scilly. The townspeople were planning a festival two weeks hence, which, for the first time in 435 years, would be attended by members of the royal family. It was a private, unpublicized visit, and only the townspeople and Scotland Yard knew that the prince and princess of Wales and their two children would be staying at Castle Dunellen during the two-day festival.

At least, that was what they had believed until the frighteningly active terrorist grapevine picked up on the news and contacted Buckingham Palace with the threat to blow up Castle Dunellen and its inhabitants if the royal couple ventured to Cornwall without first arranging the release of certain political prisoners held in English jails.

Scotland Yard was doing its best to try to track down the would-be terrorists—believed to be a faction of an antiroyal group of left-wing extremists with ties to the Middle East—but it was up to Ryder to come up with a foolproof plan to protect the young couple and their children while they were on St. Margaret. To this end, he had been brought to Cornwall twice in one week to work on the system in different "safe" locations.

As if the pressure inherent in that job weren't enough, he was finding it more and more difficult to separate his professional and personal lives. Leaving Joanna in New York when the first summons came from Scotland Yard had been difficult enough; leaving her again five days later had been nearly impossible. He knew he was hurting her but the one thing he couldn't do was let her go.

"Again?" Joanna had said when he broke the news of his second trip.

He made a face. "Afraid so."

"Another wayward husband, I suppose?"

"Something like that."

She pushed the covers aside and reached for her robe on the chair next to the bed. "I'll be leaving so you can pack."

He grabbed her wrist. "Joanna, I don't think you understand."

She laughed low in her throat. "Oh, I understand, Ryder. Duty calls. The whirlwind life of a computer whiz or detective or whatever the hell you are."

The expression in her beautiful eyes tore at his heart. "I don't want to leave you, Jo. You must know that."

She arched a dark brow. "Must I? You do it often enough."

"I wish I could stay."

She turned to face him, her breasts barely covered by the

light cashmere robe. "Then do it," she said, challenging him. "Let Alistair do whatever has to be done."

"It's not that easy."

"I didn't think so." That look of caution he'd thought was banished forever returned to her lovely face. "Go," she said. "Do whatever it is you have to do."

He drew her into his arms but her body was all sharp angles against his. The yielding softness of moments before was gone.

"You're making this harder than it has to be, Joanna," he whispered against her ear. "I'm not like your husband. I won't hurt you." This was love as he'd never experienced it before—and never would again.

"Then stay," she said, her voice fierce. "Prove it to me, Ryder. Prove it to me by staying."

But he couldn't stay. He had promises to keep both to PAX and to himself, and until those commitments had been fulfilled, all he could offer Joanna was less than the best he could be.

Of course, he could explain none of this to Joanna, who had accepted his departure with a calm anger that unnerved the hell out of him. The look on her face when she said goodbye to him at the door was the look of a woman who'd had her worst suspicions confirmed.

He wasn't entirely sure that she was wrong.

"The chopper's ready to fly us back to Heathrow."

Alistair's voice called Ryder back from his thoughts. Ryder looked up from the intricate maze of wiring in front of him. Alistair, his face ruddy and damp from the seaswept wind outside the cottage, was sitting opposite him at the table.

"When did you get in here?"

"About five minutes ago." The older man shrugged out of his waterproof parka and reached for the carafe of coffee on the table. "Your powers of concentration are phenomenal, my boy. Is the work that compelling?"

"No. It's not." Ryder was feeling too emotionally vulnerable to hide behind a flip remark.

Alistair leaned forward, his blue eyes reflecting his concern.

"Anything I can do to help? I may not be a genius, but I've been known to handle a few difficulties in my time."

For fifteen years Alistair Chambers had been friend and mentor and associate. Ryder had always known that he was the son Alistair and Sarah had wanted but never had and the burden of that privilege rested lightly across his shoulders. Today, as he sat there wondering what in hell he was going to do about Joanna, he felt the need to turn to Alistair as a son turned to a father.

As Ryder would have turned to his own father had he ever been lucky enough to know him.

He took a deep breath. "I'm in love with Joanna Stratton."

Alistair nodded. "I thought so."

"You don't look surprised."

"I'm not."

"Have I been that obvious?"

"Afraid so," Alistair said. "Even geniuses can't run from love forever."

"It's an impossible situation," Ryder said. "I thought I could have it all."

"And you're not certain of that any longer?"

"You were right, Chambers. We all have to make compromises." He dragged his hands through his hair. "In this business, a personal life is the first to go."

Alistair said nothing but the look of compassion in his eyes told Ryder everything.

"How did you and Sarah make it work?" Ryder asked, leaning forward once again. Alistair was one of the founders of PAX and Ryder knew his association with the organization predated his marriage. "Why could you marry a civilian and make it work when the rest of us can't even cope with much more than one-night stands?"

"Are you telling me you don't know?"

Ryder stared at him, confused. "Don't know what? You had a secret Haitian love potion that kept her your slave forever?"

The unflappable Alistair Chambers looked decidedly

flapped as he shifted position in his chair. "Sarah wasn't a civilian, Ryder. She was part of PAX."

Ryder's mind went totally blank as he stared across the table at the older man. "She was what?"

"Sarah was part of PAX."

Ryder leaned back until his chair was balanced on two legs. "Good try, Chambers. You had me going there for a while."

But the expression on Alistair's face didn't waver. "I'm not joking, Ryder."

He thought of Sarah McBride Chambers, the beautiful Irishwoman Alistair had adored until the day she died.

"Sarah was a housewife," Ryder said.

"Sarah was a cryptographer," Alistair countered, his eyes never leaving Ryder's. "The most brilliant cryptographer the West has ever produced."

Ryder felt as if the ground beneath him suddenly tilted. "She never traveled. She almost never left your apartments in London."

Alistair smiled fondly. "She never had to. All the equipment she needed to break the most sophisticated of codes was stored in her head."

"I always wondered how you explained your absences to Sarah."

"I never had to. She usually knew what was happening before I did."

A wave of envy washed over Ryder. "You lucky bastard," he said quietly. "You managed to have it all."

"For a while." Alistair's smile faded. "For a while I really did."

"Want to tell me why all the operatives I meet are men?"

"The luck of the draw," Alistair said. "Most of the covers are as foolproof as Sarah's. You'd never know a PAX operative if he or she didn't want you to know."

"Is Joanna an operative?" A one-in-a-million shot, but he had to ask.

"Afraid not. She's exactly what you know her to be, Ryder, and nothing more."

"That's what I was afraid of."

Joanna was the woman he loved.

And the woman he was going to lose.

Chapter Eighteen

Ryder poured himself two fingers of Scotch and stared out at Central Park. Twilight tinged the tops of the trees with dusky blue, softening the big city reality of the scene. He stood there and watched it grow dark.

In a little while he was supposed to pick up Joanna for an evening out in the company of Alistair and Holland. It had seemed a good idea at the time, the four of them going out for dinner and dancing at a trendy downtown night spot.

Now he thought the idea stank.

The only thing that did appeal to him was downing a few more glasses of Scotch in rapid succession until he got rip-roaring drunk.

But, try as he might, he couldn't avoid the one basic truth he'd been dodging for days: He had no business being there in New York.

No business at all.

The situation in Cornwall was getting hotter by the second. If he had any brains he would be back there measuring and plotting and planning the different security systems he intended to put into play during the visit of the prince and princess of Wales to the Cornish coast next week.

Even the unconfirmed rumor that the royals might be moving their trip up three days did nothing to goad him into action.

Right or wrong, the need to be near Joanna was greater than anything else in his life at the moment. For the first time in his career he had lost his concentration, his timing, the elusive edge that kept him the best in the business.

Well, the best in the business was having a hell of a time keeping his head above water right now, and it had damned little to do with Cornwall or the royal family or PAX.

He hadn't been back in Joanna's arms for more than five minutes before he realized something had changed. Where before she'd been feisty and passionate both, now only the passion remained. The high-spiritedness had turned to something more distant, more melancholy.

Something that was making him nervous as hell.

Just that afternoon he'd been picking out a highbrow version of *Chopsticks* on her mother's piano when Joanna received a phone call. Normally he wasn't the eavesdropping type—except professionally—but he'd allowed himself to pause in his mock concerto long enough to hear that it was Benny Ryan and to know she was on the verge of making a serious career move.

A move that didn't include him.

Gut instincts honed by years in a dangerous business told him that this was going to be the night she said goodbye. He wasn't a fool, and he knew that in a few short weeks they'd traveled farther than most couples traveled in a lifetime. They'd worked together; they'd faced danger; they'd loved in a way he'd never know again.

The next step was something lasting, a commitment to equal the powerful love and longing that tore at his heart. It was what he wanted; it was what she deserved.

It was the one thing he couldn't do.

The indicator on the SS543 information retriever sounded a series of three rapid tones, which signaled an urgent message too classified to go through regular channels. It meant checking the data base, scrambling the codes, then mixing the headline of that day's *New York Times* through his computer in order simply to come up with the access code necessary to begin the decoding process.

Three more tones filled the room, followed by four more,

louder this time. He was due on Joanna's doorstep in less than five minutes. Retrieving the message would take at least an hour.

Something inside him broke free, and he picked up a bookend from the shelf over the fireplace and hurled it at the expensive hunk of machinery across the room. The sound of the crash made him feel terrific.

To hell with PAX.

If it was so damned important, let them contact Alistair. There would be other nights for Alistair and Holland but for Ryder and Joanna there was only tonight.

And he'd be damned if he'd let any force in heaven or hell take that night away from him.

FINALITY WAS in the air.

Joanna could feel it in her bones. Even their lovemaking—wonderful though it was—carried within it the essence of goodbye.

It was only a matter of who said it first, and Joanna had decided that she would be the one.

And tonight would be the night.

They were doubling with Alistair and Holland and dining at an inn down near Princeton, New Jersey, where Holland was filming a small part on a new nighttime soap about sex and academia. Holland was as excited as a high school girl about the evening and, for her sake, Joanna was going to go along with their plans.

There would be plenty of time when they got home to tell Ryder of her decision.

She yanked her favorite dress out of the closet and held it up to herself before the mirror. It was a simple sheath made extraordinary by the thousands of black and silver beads painstakingly sewn to every square inch of fabric. It shimmered like moonlight in a midnight sky.

The perfect dress for saying goodbye.

Not that Ryder didn't see it coming, though. She was certain he'd been waiting for this. In fact, he would probably welcome it. The need for goodbye had been in his eyes every moment since he returned from whatever secret place he'd been.

Where he'd been brash and outspoken before, he was calm and cool now. Where energy had crackled from every pore, a strange lassitude remained.

Something had happened while he was away, something profound. Something he wasn't about to share with Joanna, no matter how much he said he loved her, no matter how badly she wanted to believe.

She slipped the dress over her head, then fumbled behind her for the zipper.

So this, then, was it. She'd made up her mind and at least took a measure of comfort from the fact that the decision this time was hers and hers alone.

Her work for Benny Ryan on the bank commercial had been a rousing success and had attracted the attention of an independent producer, who wanted Joanna to travel to Tahiti, all expenses paid, on an eight-week location shoot for *Vogue* magazine, which was about to venture into the murky waters of home video.

When they'd worked together on nailing Stanley Holt, she'd had a taste of how wonderful teaming up with Ryder could be. They'd been true partners, equals, their talents and weaknesses dovetailing so perfectly that they functioned like a precision instrument. But that partnership had disappeared the second they had the goods on Stanley.

What they had now was a pale imitation of what they'd shared, and she'd rather do without than be reminded of what could have been.

The doorbell rang and she slipped on her shoes and took one final look at herself in the mirror before she went to let him in.

Yes, she would tell Ryder tonight and, with any luck, she'd be on a Tahiti-bound plane tomorrow before he had a chance to see her cry.

IF IT HADN'T BEEN for Alistair and his continental gift of gab, Ryder doubted if he and Joanna would have made it to the corner of West 71st Street before the subject of goodbye came up. Alistair was telling her about his experience with the queen mother at a charity auction in Surrey and Joanna was laughing for the first time in days.

It was a good story, but Ryder was hard put to get his concentration back on target. Each time he tried to interject an anecdote, the damned receiver in his earlobe blasted him with a tone that made his fillings vibrate. It was a miracle Joanna hadn't heard it.

If Alistair knew about a possible emergency, he was being pretty damned cool about it. Ryder decided to do the same. One night in fifteen years wasn't a hell of a lot to ask.

The Rolls was easing its way over the Outerbridge Crossing that led from Staten Island to New Jersey. Alistair had rapped on the window separating the driver from the passenger compartment and was giving instructions on where to pick up Holland. Joanna was looking down at her manicure. The car was silent but for the low purr of the engine.

Of course, that was when PAX decided to signal with an ear-splitting blast that probably sent dogs in the tristate area out into their front yards to howl at the moon.

Joanna's head popped up. "What was that?"

He tried to look innocent. "What was what?"

Another ear splitter.

"That noise."

"I didn't hear anything."

She leaned closer to him. "You'd have to be deaf not to—there it is again! Ryder, what's going on?"

He shrugged, hoping against hope that Alistair would see fit to become involved in a long conversation with the chauffeur. "Probably a foghorn in the distance," he said, pointing to the water below the bridge. "You hear them all the time."

They eased off the Outerbridge and headed toward the New Jersey Turnpike south to Princeton.

The words "Code 33" made his mandible rattle.

"Is something wrong, Joanna?" Alistair turned back to both of them.

"I think I'm going crazy," she said with an apologetic laugh. "First I was hearing foghorns; now I'm hearing voices."

Alistair's sharp blue eyes zeroed in on Ryder. "Are you hearing voices, as well, O'Neal?"

You know damn well I am. Ryder hadn't known Alistair was quite this accomplished an actor. "You haven't heard any?" he asked, trying to keep his tone of voice light and breezy. "You usually hear them first." Joanna's eyes were wide with curiosity. He looked down at her. "Chambers is the one with the good imagination."

Alistair, however, didn't laugh. "Sometimes I get bad reception on my radio," he said, never taking his eyes from Ryder. "That's when I rely on Ryder for my information."

Ice formed in the pit of Ryder's stomach. "You haven't heard today's news?" This couldn't be happening. In fifteen years, Alistair had always been the first to know everything.

Joanna's attention swiveled from Ryder to Alistair, then back to Ryder again. She looked as if she'd rather take her chances hitchhiking on the New Jersey Turnpike than spend another minute in that Rolls.

He didn't blame her.

"Is there something I should know?" Alistair asked, the epitome of urbane calm. Only Ryder was aware of the power beneath the smile. "Perhaps the headline of *The New York Times?"*

Before Ryder had a chance to answer, all hell broke loose.

JOANNA WAS FIDDLING with the cellular telephone on the side wall of the Rolls-Royce and trying to ignore the tension between the two men when it happened.

A deep rhythmic alarm filled the air. There was no doubt that it originated right there in the limousine. She turned to Ryder. His face had drained of color. Alistair punched a series of buttons on the console near the bar, and the driver smoothly steered across three lanes of traffic onto the shoulder of the Turnpike, then rolled to a stop.

Before she could form a coherent question, a voice filled the car, booming out from the speakers on both rear doors.

"Hampshire 322," it said in a flat Midwestern tone. "Mayday Picadilly 114...Midnight stat."

A nervous laugh rippled through her. "What on earth...?"

The laughter stopped abruptly, caught by her rising fear. No one else in the limousine had even cracked a smile. Sweat popped out behind her neck and she clasped her hands together on her lap to keep them from shaking.

"Ryder, I—" She stopped when she realized he didn't even remember she existed.

My God, she thought. *He doesn't even hear me.* His fingers on the console were a blur as he punched in number after number, while Alistair recited a string of unconnected words into a microphone that uncoiled from the roof of the car like an oxygen mask on a 747.

She wished it were an oxygen mask because she was finding it hard to draw in a deep breath. The limousine merged onto the turnpike again and began racing back toward Manhattan at a clip approaching the speed of light. Suddenly all of her and Holland's half-baked suspicions about Ryder and Alistair seemed frighteningly close to reality.

For a woman who never cried, she was close to tears for the second time in as many days. Apparently Alistair recognized her panic because he reached over and patted her hand.

"We cannot let you go, you understand," he said in his cool and collected British voice. "I wish we could but it just is not possible."

"Where are we going?" she asked, looking directly at Ryder.

"Alas, I can't tell you," Alistair answered. "Company policy, you know."

At that moment, Joanna didn't know anything at all. All she wanted was to escape. She grabbed for the door handle and tugged but the damned thing was locked—which was just as well, because jumping from a moving limousine wasn't one of her more brilliant ideas.

Then she saw the revolver balanced on Ryder's thigh, and suddenly she wasn't sure that a slow death was any better.

NEXT TO HIM, Joanna was hyperventilating, and Ryder was torn between loyalty to PAX and his love for her. The Rolls was monitored by a sophisticated electronic surveillance system that could pick up a flea's whisper so he didn't dare risk even a partial explanation of what was happening.

From the code words he heard when the alarm came in, Ryder had a pretty good idea what was happening: a major crisis involving the royal family, one involving life and death.

Not that it came as any surprise.

Those warnings he'd ignored had been the first stage. If he hadn't turned his back on fifteen years of training, they might not now be racing for JFK and PAX's private Concorde.

If he hadn't turned his back, Joanna wouldn't be sitting next to him, her eyes wide with fear, wondering exactly what kind of bastard he really was.

He couldn't tell her exactly what was happening, but he could do something to alleviate her terror. He owed her that much.

Grabbing a piece of paper from the inlaid desktop adjacent to his seat, he scribbled, "Trust me, Jo. We're the good guys," and prayed that, just this once, she'd be able to put aside her suspicions and rely on blind faith.

It was a tall order.

He wouldn't blame her if she told him to go to hell.

Chapter Nineteen

The house was huge, cold and unbearably damp.

The icy chill from the North Atlantic whistled through the room where Joanna sat, waiting for Ryder or Alistair to tell her what in hell was going on.

They were on a small island, just off Cornwall, that much she knew even before she heard the unmistakable accent of the man who picked them up at the tiny airstrip.

Those massive cliffs rising above an iron-gray sea could be found no other place on earth.

Now she was seated before a stone fireplace, her wrists manacled to the arms of the chair, while Ryder, Alistair and four other men she'd never seen before huddled over the long table against the far wall and talked in a strange kind of verbal shorthand that bordered on a code.

Part of the code, however, was terrifyingly easy to understand.

The prince and princess of Wales were arriving that night for an unpublicized visit. Unfortunately, a terrorist organization had gotten wind of this trip and were threatening to blow up the children's hospital when the princess made her appearance the following afternoon.

All of the men in this room were looking toward Ryder O'Neal for a solution.

This was no rich man's son, no run-of-the-mill private investigator. The offbeat, carefree man she'd met hid another man who was driven by deeper needs, higher goals. A man whose genius had taken him farther than most men could dream.

A man she could love for all time.

She hadn't been wrong about him; she hadn't been blinded by his beauty or deaf to the memories of past hurts that had pounded in her head every day since Eddie died. All these years of doubting her own judgment, of doubting her own self-worth were over.

She wasn't a woman like her mother, destined to make the wrong choice over and over again. She didn't need a man to be complete; she didn't need a husband to prove herself a woman of value.

She was Joanna Stratton, a thirty-two-year-old woman who had finally figured out exactly what she wanted out of life.

She wanted to share her life with Ryder O'Neal, because, short of paradise, she could imagine no greater joy.

Alistair outlined the impossibility of allowing the princess to actually visit the hospital the next day, and Joanna was reminded that there was still a terrifying reality to be dealt with before any of her fantasies could possibly come true.

"We cannot chance it," Alistair said, his cultured tones rising over the sound of the wind that slammed against the rocks below the house. "The risk to her life is too great."

Ryder stood up and leaned across the weathered oak table. "And what about the risk to everyone else? If we let them get away with it here, there's no place on earth that's safe." His voice was impassioned, and the other men fell silent before him. "The hospital is an enclosed position with easily defensible perimeters. If we're ever going to have a chance to nail those bastards, this is it."

"Impossible," a slender, dark-haired man with manicured fingernails said. "No grandstand plays in our district. I shan't allow it."

"Agreed," said the man with the shaggy gray beard and horn-rimmed glasses. "If you fail, O'Neal, it is we who bear the mark of shame."

What was the matter with these men that they couldn't see the wisdom of Ryder's plan? Risk was all; nothing valuable in life ever came easy.

Including love.

Where had her doubts and fears disappeared to? Any normal woman would be terrified, trapped somewhere on the Cornish coast with a man who'd turned out to be some kind of high-tech spy. Less than twenty-four hours ago, Joanna herself was wishing Ryder O'Neal were a high school teacher or a shoe salesman—someone upon whom she could depend.

Now she wondered how she could have been so narrow in her thinking, so fearful of the unknown. He was everything she'd ever wanted in a man and more, because he understood the meaning of the word, commitment, in a way few others could.

And even if she never saw him again once this adventure was over, even if her dreams of forever after proved no more than that, she'd never be sorry that, for a little while, she'd given him her heart.

"It is their decision, Ryder," Alistair said, rubbing the bridge of his nose with thumb and forefinger. "We must abide by it."

Ryder was a man possessed. "Terrific," he said, slamming his fist down on the tabletop. "And when we're through watching them destroy the royal family, we can sit back and watch them go for the President of the United States. Sounds great."

The bearded man chuckled nervously. "You Americans always manage to bring the facts back home, don't you?"

Her admiration soared as Ryder refused to give an inch. "Have you people lived with terrorism so long you've forgotten how to fight it?" he asked. "Damn it to hell! If we don't take a stand now, we'll all lose."

Joanna watched as Alistair placed a restraining hand on Ryder's forearm. "The stand cannot include risking the princess's life," he said. "The danger is too real; the loss would be too devastating."

Ryder wasn't in the mood, however, to listen to reason. "Doesn't anyone understand a damned thing I'm saying? There is no risk—with my equipment, we can detect and defuse plastic explosives before they have a chance to be detonated."

He talked of nitrogen compounds and electrophilic properties and free electrons, and suddenly something clicked inside Joanna.

This was her chance to be part of something important, to finally take her skills and stretch her talent to the limit. This was her chance to sample what the future would be like with a man like Ryder O'Neal.

"I understand." Joanna's voice echoed in the enormous room. "I understand and I think I can help."

The rest was up to him.

IN HIS ENTIRE LIFE, Ryder O'Neal had never known a sweeter moment.

Joanna's words echoed throughout the room—and inside his heart. It didn't matter that the other men, Alistair included, stared at her as if she'd just escaped from a psychiatric prison—he knew what it had cost her to volunteer, and in that moment he was lost forever.

Forget his notion of goodbye. Forget his plans to shield her from his uncertain life, to protect her from heartbreak the way he'd failed to protect Valerie a long, long time ago.

Forget everything but the incredible, towering rush of pleasure that buoyed him skyward as he realized he was about to share the deepest part of himself with the woman who had stolen both his heart and his soul.

Joanna Stratton had volunteered to call upon all of her skills in order to take the place of the princess of Wales and tour the children's hospital tomorrow. She would be putting her life right there on the line, relying on nothing more than her faith in Ryder to keep her safe.

No words of love, no secret music in the dark of the night could have better told him how she felt.

"Who is she?" protested John Chaney, adjusting the lapels on his suit. "Who brought that woman here?"

"Total insanity," muttered Leonard Williams, tugging on his beard as he stared across the room at Joanna, who managed to look regal even in handcuffs. "Just bring in the bobbies and rely on an old-fashioned show of strength."

Alistair Chambers, mentor and friend, said nothing. He just poured himself another Scotch and sat back to watch the inevitable unfold. The fact that he'd completed work on the detection prototype wasn't the only secret Ryder had been keeping.

Ryder bent down in front of Joanna and unlocked the handcuffs. Those beautiful blue-green eyes of hers watched as he pressed his lips to her wrists, which bore red marks where the metal had dug into her flesh.

"If you say yes, there's no turning back, Joanna."

Her gaze didn't waver. "I won't want to turn back."

"My prototype's never been tried. There's no guarantee."

A smile darted across her face, then disappeared. "I've learned that life doesn't come with guarantees."

"You're putting yourself in a hell of a lot of danger."

"I trust you," she said. "That's all I need to know."

Those words were words he had never thought to hear, words he had never thought himself worthy of. But he looked at her lovely and serious face and knew that she was incapable of anything less than the truth, incapable of giving him less than everything she had.

A man could spend a lifetime with a woman like that.

If things went well tomorrow, he intended to do exactly that.

Alistair's discreet cough snagged their attention.

"The brass will never believe you didn't have this planned," he said, looking from Ryder to Joanna and back again. "How convenient to have a woman of Ms. Stratton's technical skills at our disposal."

"The luck of the draw," Ryder said, forgetting the fact that he'd ignored PAX's warning signal.

"Fortunate timing," said Joanna.

"You realize that what happens here, dies here," Alistair said, focusing in on Joanna. "If you'll pardon the clumsy phraseology. Once we leave Cornwall, it is as if this never happened."

Joanna's eyes were wide and innocent. "I have a terrible memory," she said sweetly. "It's a major flaw."

Alistair sighed, deep and long. "I don't suppose I can convince the two of you to take the easy way out, can I?"

Ryder looked toward Joanna. He wouldn't have blamed her if she decided to back out but, damned if she didn't meet Alistair's gaze head-on.

Ryder felt as if she'd lassoed the sun and moon and stars and laid them at his feet.

"Sorry," she said, her voice firm. "I'm in for the long haul."

Joanna Stratton, he thought, *when this is over, I'm going to hold you to that.*

JOANNA HAD ONE shaky moment that afternoon when the princess of Wales and her entourage entered the makeshift studio where Joanna would be casting the life mask that would be the basis of her own transformation.

The princess was understandably tense; the effects of the threat of terrorism against her family showed in the circles beneath her cornflower-blue eyes and in the way she fiddled constantly with the sapphire and diamond band on her left hand.

Joanna was rarely awed by celebrities of any kind, but royalty was an exception. Being this close to the most popular luminary of the twentieth century had her tongue-tied at first. Only the princess's genuine interest in Joanna and her craft eased Joanna's stage fright and got her back on track once again.

Now dress rehearsals were over and in a little more than two hours, Joanna would be taking center stage.

The latex mask, cast with the princess's own patrician features, was ready to be donned. The trademark blond wig rested on a stand near the makeup mirror. Joanna was already dressed in one of the princess's elegant red wool suits that a royal seamstress had quickly altered to accommodate Joanna's wider American shoulders and fuller breasts.

She touched the huge button earrings Ryder had given her. They were trendy and totally in keeping with the royal image. No one would suspect that they were the first line of defense in tracking down the terrorists.

She would never understand the manipulation of ions and sound waves that Ryder outlined to her when he explained the technology behind his invention; she didn't need to. All she needed to know was that the second she heard the low hum in her left ear, she was to signal Ryder—who would be acting as royal bodyguard—by adjusting the angle of her hat.

What happened after that was anyone's guess.

IF RYDER DIDN'T KNOW the truth, he would think the princess of Wales had thought better of the idea, and decided to visit the St. Margaret Hospital for Children after all.

The transformation was that complete. The only clue that Joanna Stratton was hidden beneath the blond bob and the impeccable tailoring was the way she gripped his hand in the limousine before they pulled up in front of the hospital.

However, the second they exited and faced the cheering crowd of islanders lining the paved walkway, Joanna was every inch the princess. The smile, the slight incline of the head, the wave—all were the patented property of the princess of Wales.

He would defy even the prince to tell the difference—at least from a respectful distance.

Joanna blinked rapidly and met Ryder's eyes for an instant. Alistair was probably broadcasting her final instructions through the tiny transmitter embedded in her earlobe, the same as his. It had taken Ryder six months to get used to this blatant invasion of privacy; Joanna acted as if she were born to the life.

Don't kid yourself, he thought. This was the glamorous part, the fun part. The part that made it hard to think of returning to real life.

Once they entered that hospital, Joanna's life was on the line. The terrorist group had contacted Buckingham Palace just two hours ago in response to Parliament's refusal to release the political prisoners demanded by the terrorists.

"She dies," the spokesman said. "And you cannot stop us."

If he had to go to hell and back, Ryder O'Neal would stop them.

Mrs. Penhaligon, head of the hospital, curtsied in front of Joanna. "My staff awaits your visit, Your Highness. This is the most exciting thing to ever happen here on St. Margaret."

Joanna smiled and Ryder swallowed down his fear and followed them into the hospital.

From your mouth to God's ear, Mrs. Penhaligon.

Chapter Twenty

Princesses didn't sweat.

Any woman raised on a diet of fairy tales knew that for a fact.

However, at that moment Joanna would have bet her borrowed tiara that very few princesses could find themselves in a situation such as this and not work up at least a ladylike glow.

She casually swept a hand beneath her blond bangs and caught the beads of perspiration that had worked their way out from under the heavy wig. During the past hour in the surgical ward of the children's hospital, Joanna had accepted twelve bouquets of flowers, six proposals of marriage and four invitations to stop round the cottage for dinner.

The people, adults and children alike, loved the princess of Wales with a love that bordered on devotion. Protocol was forgotten about as small hands clutched at her skirt and larger hands reached out to clasp her own. She was a link to past glories and a bridge to future triumphs. What happened to her and her young family mattered.

Ryder's silent presence beside her—and the knowledge that he carried more firearms on his person than she'd ever seen in her entire life—seemed ludicrous. Certainly none of these open-faced, smiling people could be planning a mass murder.

"There is one more ward, Your Highness," said Alistair, looking over the head of Mrs. Penhaligon. His blue eyes were grave and steady. "I think you will enjoy the children on this one."

Joanna nodded. One more ward. Five minutes, eight at most, and they'd be home free. She swallowed hard as they approached the room at the end of the hallway.

The pediatric ambulatory ward was crowded with children. Children on crutches, children in wheelchairs, children sitting primly at maple play tables waiting for a glimpse of the princess.

Murals of Big Bird and Ernie graced one wall, proof that some truths were indeed universal. A fire snapped and crackled merrily in the grate, and Joanna could no more believe this room harbored danger than she could believe in the tooth fairy.

She moved ahead of Ryder toward the group of kids sitting on the end of the first bed by the window. Their smiles lit up the room; she was amazed that just a simple pat on the head or hug could make such a difference in so many lives.

She bent down to look at one particularly pretty little red-haired girl. If they hadn't come up with the laryngitis excuse, she could have spent the rest of the day sitting there telling them stories.

Joanna's job kept her on the run—in strange places with even stranger people—and so she was rarely around children. She'd forgotten just how wonderful it would be to relive the adventures of Jack the Giant Killer, and Snow White and—

A flash of movement from the corner of the room. She glanced at Ryder and he motioned for her to stay put. Nothing seemed unusual about the scene: two doctors with stethoscopes around their necks leaned against the doorjamb; an orderly stared at Joanna as if she were descended from the stars; a nurse, hands in pockets, looked out the window toward the cliffs two stories below.

Nothing to worry about.

But, wait. Where everyone else's uniform had a thin navy stripe outlining the collar, this nurse had none. And, if Joanna's eyes weren't playing tricks on her, a thin piece of wire trailed from the nurse's right ear and disappeared into the bodice of the uniform.

Joanna started toward her.

It might be nothing.

It probably *was* nothing.

Perhaps the woman was one of Ryder's mysterious cohorts that she had yet to meet, or the wire belonged to nothing more ominous than a hearing aid.

Joanna took a deep breath as she closed in on the nurse, whose back was still to her. No more than twelve feet separated them.

In a few moments, this would all be over and Ryder and Alistair and the rest of their organization could relax, knowing that the threat against the princess of Wales had been an empty one.

Eight feet. Seven. Six—

A sound. Deep, throbbing, unmistakable even though she was hearing it for the first time. The entire left side of her face pounded with it and she stopped in her tracks, her hand resting over the enormous earring-cum-alarm system.

Dear God! If the alarm blaring in her ear were any indication, the woman in front of her was wired with enough plastic explosives to blast them all the way back to London.

Ryder flanked her left side; Alistair and two other associates flanked her right. The alarm intensified. She could barely think.

The signal. What in hell was the signal?

The nurse turned around. Joanna met her eyes and saw evil face-to-face for the first time.

Her hand flew to the brim of her hat, and Ryder threw her to the ground while Alistair and the other two men turned what looked to be Uzi machine guns on the nurse. Instead of raining bullets, the machine guns rained a thick, viscous yellow substance that clung to the terrorist like mucilage.

"The kids," Ryder yelled. "Get them out now."

"But it's over," she said. "You've neutralized the plastics. We're safe."

The danger was past. The good guys had won. She was in Ryder's arms. Everything was over except the happy ending.

That was when she realized it wasn't over at all. There, in front of her, stood the terrorist, looking like an apparition from the worst of the horror movies Joanna had ever worked on. While Joanna watched, the woman extracted a live bomb from a spot beneath the window.

The old-fashioned kind.

The kind that ticked.

"Back away!" The woman's voice was heavy with the sound of the Middle East.

To Joanna's surprise, Alistair and the other men complied instantly. Ryder remained positioned over Joanna, shielding her. Her heart hammered in counter-time to the ticking of the bomb.

"You move," the woman said, motioning toward Ryder. "She is the one we want."

"Listen to her," Alistair said quietly. "It's our only chance."

The room emptied of patients and hospital staff. Joanna could hear Mrs. Penhaligon sobbing in the corridor.

Ryder still didn't move. Fear made it hard for Joanna to think. The only reality in this insane nightmare was the strength and warmth of his body against hers. If he moved away from her, all of her brave talk of doing something important, of living life on the wild side, would be exposed for what it was: the talk of a woman who knew very little about the ways of the world.

"Two minutes," the terrorist screamed. "Two minutes and this building is no more."

"Use your head, son," Alistair roared. "Don't be a fool. Go near her and it's all over. She'll blow us all to hell. There are other ways to deal with this."

And then, to Joanna's horror, Ryder O'Neal got up and moved away.

Everything was over now—including the happy ending.

IT WAS every nightmare he'd ever had and refused to acknowledge in the light of day.

Love and duty. The topic of late night, whiskey-soaked talks, of speculation and uncertainty.

The one thing every operative feared.

And here it was, right here in front of him, the classic confrontation.

In the years since he walked away from Valerie Parker, he'd wondered what he would do when the ultimate conflict—choosing between the woman he loved and his commitment to duty—presented itself.

Only nothing had prepared him for the reality of standing there helpless while the woman he loved beyond duty, beyond training, beyond his own life, was being used as a pawn in a game of danger and death.

"Cover Joanna," he said to Alistair. "I'll handle this."

"Go slow," Alistair said. "Play for time. The bomb blanket is on the way."

"No talking!" the terrorist screamed. "No more talk!"

She put the small bomb inside her blouse and reached for Joanna. Something inside Ryder went mad with rage. He'd spent his life playing games, avoiding commitment, skating by on charm as much as skill.

He was through playing for time.

He grabbed for the bomb. The terrorist struggled. The bomb continued ticking.

Forty seconds. Thirty-five...

He remembered how Joanna had felt in his arms, remembered how much it had cost her to believe in him. He owed her this one, last gift: her life.

When there was no more time left at all, he grabbed the terrorist by the shoulders and the two of them crashed through the mullioned window toward the sea and the rocks below.

THE CAST ON HIS LEG LOOKED heavy and hot and it probably itched like hell, but to Joanna Stratton it was the most beautiful sight on earth.

At the moment she could think of no greater pleasure than simply watching Ryder O'Neal breathe.

"You must have nine lives," she said as PAX's private Concorde took off from Heathrow on their delayed flight back to the States. "That fall would have killed a lesser man." The luck of the Irish had been with him—not to mention high tide.

Ryder grinned and pulled her down next to him on the hospital bed Alistair had had installed for the return trip. "Eight more lives to go," he said, kissing the side of her neck. "I don't know if I can stand the excitement."

"I can," Joanna said. "If I spend those lives with you."

His hazel eyes twinkled with delight. "Is that a proposal, Ms. Stratton?"

"No," she said, pointing toward the cast. "That is."

There, in lipstick-red, the words "Will you marry me?" were scrawled along the side of the cast.

Ryder started to laugh. "When did you do that?"

"When you were napping."

"I don't nap."

"Afraid you did, Superman."

He stroked her hair gently and she marveled at the tenderness this man of power and danger was capable of. "Eight more weeks in this cast," he said. "I make a lousy patient."

"Don't change the subject."

"I just want you to know what you're getting into, Joanna. It may not always be this easy."

"This was easy?"

"I have a lousy temper."

"I know."

"I smoke cigars now and then."

"I'll buy air freshener."

"I've been known to eat cold pizza and drink warm beer."

"I'll pretend I didn't hear that."

"You probably have questions."

"A million of them," she said. "But I'll have forty or fifty years to get the answers."

He gripped Joanna by the shoulders and drew her across his chest until her eyes were level with his.

"This is your last chance to back out, Joanna."

She tilted her head toward the window. "From fifty thousand feet up? Not very likely. Besides, you wouldn't deny Rosie the chance to say I told you so."

"I love you," he said softly. "I always will."

"Now there you have me, Mr. O'Neal," Joanna said, reaching up to extinguish the overhead light. "That's something you'll just have to prove to me."

LAUGHTER.

Alistair looked up from the London daily newspaper and listened.

There was no mistaking that sound.

Low. Seductive. Wonderful.

And probably the most private of sounds on earth.

He leaned over and made sure the door between the cabins was closed, then clicked on the tape player. Strains of an old Cole Porter tune enveloped him in a haze of sweet nostalgia. He couldn't hear their laughter any longer but the sound lingered in his memory.

Ah, yes. To be young and in love...

How Sarah would have enjoyed seeing their young friend so happy. But that was neither here nor there. When they landed in New York, he would have to see about setting Ryder up with the facilities he'd wanted for his development work. And Joanna—well, Alistair would be a fool if he didn't do his damnedest to lure her into utilizing her amazing skills in some capacity for PAX.

No longer could Alistair pretend that Ryder was needed in the field. The perfect blend of love and work was there for the taking, and Alistair would make certain Ryder had his chance. No longer could Alistair ignore the fact that Ryder deserved a chance at the happiness he himself had once taken for granted.

There was a lesson to be learned there and Alistair was nothing if not a fast learner.

He put down the newspaper and picked up the air-to-ground telephone. He didn't have to check the number; he couldn't forget it if he wanted to.

"I should hang up on you, Alistair Chambers," Holland said, her voice crystal clear despite the miles separating them. "I waited ten hours for you to show up and that was three days ago. Where in hell are you? This story better be good."

"It is," he said, thinking about love and romance and how splendid it was that they were no longer solely the property of the young and the blessed. "It is."

Harlequin Romance®

Delightful

Affectionate

Romantic

Emotional

Tender

Original

Daring

Riveting

Enchanting

Adventurous

Moving

Harlequin Romance—the
series that has it all!

HROM-G

HARLEQUIN PRESENTS®

HARLEQUIN PRESENTS
men you won't be able to resist
falling in love with...

HARLEQUIN PRESENTS
women who have feelings
just like your own...

HARLEQUIN PRESENTS
powerful passion in
exotic international settings...

HARLEQUIN PRESENTS
intense, dramatic stories that will keep you
turning to the very last page...

HARLEQUIN PRESENTS
The world's bestselling romance series!

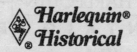

Harlequin® Historical

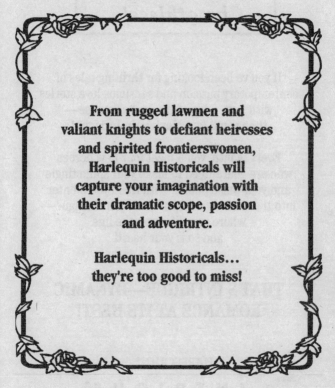

From rugged lawmen and
valiant knights to defiant heiresses
and spirited frontierswomen,
Harlequin Historicals will
capture your imagination with
their dramatic scope, passion
and adventure.

Harlequin Historicals…
they're too good to miss!

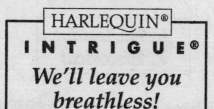

HARLEQUIN®
I N T R I G U E®

We'll leave you breathless!

If you've been looking for thrilling tales of
contemporary passion and sensuous love stories
with taut, edge-of-the-seat suspense—
then you'll *love* **Harlequin Intrigue!**

Every month, you'll meet four new heroes
who are guaranteed to make your spine tingle
and your pulse pound. With them you'll enter
into the exciting world of Harlequin Intrigue—
where your life is on the line
and so is your heart!

THAT'S INTRIGUE—DYNAMIC ROMANCE AT ITS BEST!

HARLEQUIN®

I N T R I G U E®